Crimean Fig/
Qırım İnciri

ARROWSMITH
PRESS

Crimean Fig/Qırım İnciri

ISBN: 979-8-9915254-8-0

Boston — New York — San Francisco — Baghdad
San Juan — Kyiv — Istanbul — Santiago, Chile
Beijing — Paris — London — Cairo — Madrid
Milan — Melbourne — Jerusalem — Darfur

11 Chestnut St.
Medford, MA 02155
arrowsmithpress@gmail.com
www.arrowsmithpress.com

The sixty-seventh Arrowsmith book was typeset & designed by Bella Bennett
for Askold Melnyczuk & Alex Johnson in Plantin.

Crimean Fig/
Qırım İnciri

Anastasia Levkova

Askold Melnyczuk

Nataliya Shpylova-Saeed

Contents

Plucking the First Crimean Figs

Askold Melnyczuk

Shortly after Russia invaded Ukraine on February 24, 2022, I began recording interviews with Ukrainian writers. All too aware of Ukraine's experience in the first half of the twentieth century, when entire generations of Ukrainian intellectuals were wiped out by Stalin and company, I wanted to be sure the world knew something about the people under siege. Several of these writers—Yuri Andrukhovych and Marjana Savka—I'd known a long time. I'd met Yuri back in 1990 when I attended a poetry conference in Kyiv just before the dissolution of the Soviet Union. I came to know Marjana while she was in residence at the Joiner Center for the Study of War and Social Consequences. I had even translated some of her poems. Others, like Yuliya Musakovska and Olena Huseinova, I'd met only in passing at book festivals in Ukraine. Still others—Kateryna Mikhailitsyna, Pavlo Korubchak, Iryna Shuvalova, and Lyuba Yakimchuk—had been recommended to me by mutual friends.

I believe it was Tetyana Teren who suggested I speak to Alim Aliev, a journalist and human rights worker, who at the time was working as deputy director of the Ukrainian Institute. Alim is co-author of

Mustafa Dzhemilev: Unbreakable, about the legendary Crimean Tatar leader, former Soviet dissident, and current member of the Ukrainian Parliament, who conducted the longest hunger strike in the history of the human rights movement. Born in Uzbekistan, to which his family had been deported from Crimea in 1944, Alim had previously been program director at "Crimea House," an organization devoted to monitoring the rights of all the peninsula's citizens.

From Alim I learned about Stalin's deportation of almost the entire indigenous Crimean Tatar population of Crimea. Nearly half the deportees died along the way to their new "home" in Central Asia. After Ukrainian independence in 1991, Crimean Tatars began returning to their homes.

Many aspects of Alim's experience evoked stories I heard from my own family growing up. This included the intense yearning his parents continued to feel for their native land even after decades.

When I asked where I might be able to read contemporary Crimean Tatar literary work, I was stunned to discover that virtually nothing was available in English. And so was born the idea for this anthology.

Thanks to Alim, I connected with the remarkable Ukrainian writer and activist Anastasia Levkova. The Crimean Tatar language is listed as one of the most endangered on the planet. Among Anastasia's projects was the development of a contest for Crimean Tatar writers under the heading "Crimean Fig." Anastasia took on herself the task of soliciting contributions from Crimean Tatar writers for our anthology. Anastasia in turn brought us to Leyla Seytkhalilova, who provided cribs from the Crimean Tatar.

There were various unexpected twists along the way—some of the writers, fearing retribution from Russian authorities, chose to withdraw their contributions. Anastasia persevered and proceeded selflessly throughout the process.

Once we had all the materials we needed, I then decided to follow the method I'd used when co-editing *From Three Worlds,* an anthology of fiction and poetry by the generation of Ukrainian writers who came of age in the 1980s. English-language cribs were distributed to gifted young American writers (in the case of the earlier anthology, these writers included Jumpha Lahiri, Lloyd Schwartz, George Packer, and

Larissa Szporluk, among others) who proceeded to render them into a contemporary American idiom. These versions were then further tweaked by a committed group of proofreaders.

The stories and poems assembled here are shadowed by history. Inevitably, they reflect the traumas endured by Crimean Tatars over the last three and a half centuries. They further chronicle the complex process of a population's efforts at reintegration into an ancestral land from which they'd been exiled over more than half a century. One hears, in both the stories and poems, a cultural and national pride, love for a land of stunning natural beauty, and a longing for the stability of peace.

What follows is the result of the collective effort of a great many writers—from Crimea, Ukraine, the United States, and India. To all of them I offer my deepest thanks.

This anthology could not have come together as it has without the committed support of my co-editor, Nataliya Shpylova-Saeed. She engaged the project wholeheartedly and raised the level for everyone.

My thanks, first, to all the writers who entrusted us with their work, to Alim Aliev, Anastasia Levkova, Leyla Seytkhalilova, and all our translators, as well as to the team of meticulous proofreaders at Arrowsmith Press.

We recognize that this book represents a modest first step in calling attention to a neglected part of the world. Our dearest wish is that other translators and publishers engage with this trove of undiscovered literature from that ancient yet enduring culture forged over centuries by the Crimean Tatars.

What Do We Know About Crimea?

Alim Aliev

A peninsula where Russia's war against Ukraine started? A territory plagued by human rights violations and the absence of justice? A battlefield of the Crimean War in the 19th century? But Crimea is more than a site of tragic events or a source of breaking news—it's an incredibly beautiful place with the sea, mountains, and steppe, a constellation of ancient civilizations, and a land of remarkable artists and scholars. Crimea is home to Crimean Tatars, Ukraine's indigenous people. They had their own state for centuries, established Zincirli Madrasa—one of the oldest educational institutions in the region—in the 15th century, and, in 1917, founded the world's first Muslim democratic republic, whose Constitution granted equal voting rights to men and women.

The history of the Crimean Tatar people over the past 242 years is one of repeated Russian colonization of the peninsula and its indigenous people's resistance to it. It all began with the annexation of Crimea by the Russian Empire in 1783 and the destruction of the Crimean Khanate, the state of the Crimean Tatars. This transformed the peninsula's political, economic, and socio-cultural life, unleashing mass persecution of the indigenous population, from the nobility to peasants. For the first time, Russians—who had never previously lived on the peninsula—began settling there. This fact undermines the Russian myth of Crimea as "historically Russian land."

The 19th century is known among Crimean Tatars as "qara asır," or "dark century." It was a time marked by the most massive wave of forced migration of indigenous people from the peninsula, triggered by the Russian Empire's defeat in the Crimean War (1853–1856). In response to its loss, Russia intensified its discriminatory policies, forcing thousands of Crimean Tatars to abandon their homes and property and migrate to the Ottoman Empire. Since then, the Crimean Tatar population abroad has consistently outnumbered those remaining on the peninsula, and this proportion still holds. Estimates suggest that between 3 and 5 million Crimean Tatars live in Turkey alone, while no more than 300 thousand reside in Crimea. For comparison, when Catherine II annexed Crimea, the region was home to over a million Crimean Tatars. By the late 19th century, that number had dwindled to fewer than 200,000.

Along with the Soviet regime, the 20th century brought yet another tragic ordeal for Crimean Tatars—the 1944 deportation. Nearly the entire population was packed into cattle cars and taken more than 1,200 miles away from Crimea over the course of almost three weeks: mostly to Uzbekistan but also to Kazakhstan, Siberia, the Urals, and elsewhere. The aftermath of this genocide was horrifying: 46 percent of the entire Crimean Tatar population died.

The deportation affected almost every family. For example, I was born in Uzbekistan, where my parents' families had been deported. However, we returned to Crimea in 1989—following 45 years of resistance through the mass non-violent Crimean Tatar movement during Soviet times. Our return and resettlement in our homeland coincided with the declaration of Ukraine's independence and the building of a young Ukrainian democracy. During this period, Crimean Tatars revived old or established new political, cultural, religious, and research institutions of their own. The process continued until February 2014, when it was interrupted by Russia's temporary occupation of Crimea.

The occupation marked Russia's cynical attempt not just to destroy the existing system of international law and destabilize the European region but also to satisfy its 21st-century imperial ambitions and recolonize the peninsula and, later, other occupied territories of Ukraine. This recolonization has had specific manifestations:

- **Militarization of the peninsula.** Crimea has been rapidly transformed from a tourist paradise into a militarized zone. Defense industry facilities now operate across the peninsula, while Russia has deployed military equipment, regular army, and secret services. Since the start of the full-scale invasion, Crimea has become one of the main launch sites for Russian missile attacks on Ukraine. Another dangerous element of this process is military indoctrination, the cult of war, and the glorification of the Russian army among children and youth.

- **Destruction of Crimean Tatar national institutions.** Persecution has forced most independent media outlets to leave the peninsula and relocate to Kyiv. The Mejlis of the Crimean Tatar People, a key institution of national self-government, was banned in Crimea, labeled extremist, and its leaders were convicted and effectively declared persona non-grata on the peninsula. This crackdown was motivated by the Mejlis' open rejection of Crimea's occupation and its support for Ukraine's territorial integrity.

- **Population replacement.** Since the start of the temporary occupation, around 70 thousand Crimean Tatars left Crimea, resulting in a brain drain as proactive groups—students, entrepreneurs, public figures, journalists, artists, and scholars—left the peninsula. In their place, Russia relocated at least 800 thousand people to Crimea, accounting for one-third of the peninsula's current population.

- **Erasure of Crimean Tatar and Ukrainian identities and creation of "Russian identity" in Crimea.** The Kremlin's imperial policy deliberately targets cultural heritage—both tangible and intangible—that "does not fit" its contemporary ideology and demonstrates historical and cultural ties between Crimea and other parts of Ukraine. The study of Crimean Tatar and Ukrainian languages is being systemically curtailed despite UNESCO classifying Crimean Tatar as an endangered language. A striking example of this identity erasure is the Khan's Palace in Bakhchysarai. It is the most significant site of the tangible cultural heritage of the Crimean Tatar people. Dating back to the 16th century, it is the world's only surviving example of Crimean Tatar palace architecture. Today, it is at risk of destruction due to Russian "restoration works," which involve replacing authentic materials with modern substitutes.

Despite the modern Russian colonization of Crimea and its anti-human steamroller of repression, for all these years, the Crimean Tatars and pro-Ukrainian residents of the peninsula continue to actively resist and pursue initiatives to preserve their identity and protect their rights.

You are now holding the first English-language anthology of contemporary Crimean Tatar literature—a product of one such initiative, *Crimean Fig / Qırım İnciri*. This Ukrainian and Crimean Tatar literary project was launched in 2018 in Kyiv with the aim of promoting the development and use of the Crimean Tatar language and literature. It seeks to spotlight Crimea and Crimean Tatars in Ukrainian intellectual discourse and facilitate translations between the two languages, fostering deeper mutual understanding between the two cultures. The texts in this anthology embody the intellectual nerve of contemporary Crimea, which—through the language of literature—captures the uncomfortable, sometimes tragic, sometimes heroic and lyrical realities of life under occupation. They reveal the unknown chapters in the history of the peninsula and its residents, taking readers on exciting adventures and inspiring them to dream.

I would like to offer you a brief overview of Crimean Tatar literature. It has deep roots, with Mahmud Qırımlı's *Yusuf and Zuleikha* as its earliest known work, written in the 13th century. During the Crimean Khanate period, literature flourished. There was palace literature (*saray edebiyatı*), also known as "divan literature"—secular books written by khans and the nobility. Alongside it, spiritual literature addressed religious themes. Folk literature—legends, fairy tales, proverbs, lyrical, humorous, and wedding songs, and epic stories, or dastans—also thrived. I should also mention the poetry of *ashiks*, bards who traveled from town to town, from village to village playing the *saz*, a plucked string instrument, and performing verses on philosophical, social, and mystical subjects. Aşıq Ümer was one of the most prominent representatives of this genre.

After Russia's annexation in the 18th century, Crimean Tatar literature went into decline. The Russian authorities on the peninsula destroyed books, ousted Crimean Tatar language from all spheres of use, replacing it with Russian, and persecuted Crimean Tatars themselves. It was Ismail Gasprinsky, an educator, writer, and reformer, who began to revive Crimean Tatar literature in the late 19th century. He wrote fiction, a genre previously uncommon in Crimean Tatar literature, founded *Terciman,* a Crimean Tatar-language newspaper, and stood at the origins of modernist ideas in education, influencing the entire Turko-Muslim world. His name is known far beyond Crimea. Gasprinsky's followers, writers Bekir Choban-zade, Eshref Shemi-zade, Shamil Alyadin, and Yusuf Bolat, continued his legacy, laying the groundwork for contemporary Crimean Tatar literature.

During the Soviet era, Crimean Tatar literature faced another period of decline. In the 1930s, Stalin's regime intensified its persecution of political opposition, intellectuals, and cultural figures. The repression reached its peak in 1937–1938, becoming what is now known as the Great Terror. On a single day, April 17, 1938, communists murdered 36 prominent representatives of the Crimean Tatar intellectual elite. Their trials lasted no more than twenty minutes each. The Soviets charged these people with nationalism and executed all of them in three days. The genocide of 1944 nearly brought the literary process to a halt. It was not until the 1970s that authors in exile started writing about the deportation as their people's collective trauma and articulated their generation's mission—to return to their homeland.

A new literary renaissance began as Crimean Tatars returned from exile to Crimea, which coincided with the early years of Ukraine's independence. Poets, writers, and journalists who came back to their homeland hosted literary events, actively contributed to the social and political life on the peninsula, and freely published and distributed large print runs of newspapers and magazines that had circulated underground during Soviet times. The establishment of national schools, libraries, a theater, a university, and media nourished the literary process, offering it practical platforms.

Russia's temporary occupation of Crimea disrupted this process, yet again threatening the very existence of Crimean Tatar identity and subjecting public life on the peninsula to censorship. Literature has become a tiny island of freedom where authors—sometimes writing under pseudonyms—raise the issues of temporary occupation and its consequences. A new genre, "literature from behind bars," has also emerged. Crimean political prisoners, sentenced by Russia under fabricated charges, write poetry and prose from their cells in Russian and Crimean prisons. This whole tapestry of texts is published in the *Crimean Fig* anthologies. Our contributors include illegally imprisoned Server Mustafayev, Asan Akhtem, Osman Arifmemetov, Vadym Siruk, and Mumine Saliyeva, the wife of political prisoner Server Saliyev. Among the authors is also Nariman Dzhelyal, a prominent public and political figure, journalist, and first deputy head of the Mejlis of the Crimean Tatar People. Dzhelyal was illegally sentenced by the Russian regime in September 2021 and liberated in June 2024.

Crimean Fig and contemporary Crimean Tatar literature as a whole are an effective antidote to the Kremlin's imperial efforts to forcibly integrate Crimea into the destructive "Russian world."

—Alim Aliev, founder of the *Crimean Fig* literary project, member of PEN Ukraine.

The Black Walls of the Zindan[1]

Mustafa Amet

Adapted by John Fulton
and Lara Stecewycz

Dedicated to Osman, Nazmiya, and Emir

My grandmother used to say that everything has its own soul: stone, grass, water, earth, wood, and air, and even the sun, the moon, planet Earth, and each star—everything in the universe. People and animals also have souls. And with this soul, they are given life from God. My grandmother would also say, "*If there is no need, do not tear off a leaf, or move a stone from its place,*" and "*Use water only when necessary and be sure not to foul it.*" Of course, I was only a child and did not pay attention to her words. I played with the children in my street and we broke branches, pulled grass, and threw stones into the water. We did not crush or kill ants, beetles, snails, or frogs, but from time to time, we kicked a stubborn ram or goat or beat them with a stick. We were merely children; we didn't understand things. But in later years, we began to realize and regret what we'd done.

Yakup, the son of our neighbor Naile tata,[2] was my closest friend. We lived on the same street, sat in the same class at school, shared the same desk, played pranks together, and were punished together. Once, we learned from the older children where and how we could see the spirits of the earth, water, and home. They told each other scary stories about a Mermaid and we all listened and learned what we needed to do to meet her. So, one cloudless and hot summer day, while everyone was resting in their cool houses at noon, we went to the river and hid among the reeds. If the Mermaid came ashore, we'd steal her golden comb and run away. I didn't know for sure if she appeared, but as soon as we heard the reeds rustle, our hearts filled with terror and we fled.

Vivid pictures of these joyful, bright, carefree days of childhood are still with me now, and I cherish them. Plaster walls, a squat house, and a sunny yard with green trees, orchards, vines, and colorful fields surrounding my grandmother's village are now simple, unpretentious memories valuable only to me. But they keep me up at night. These memories and half-dreams give me hope, as I remain in this terrible place.

In fact, life is made up of simple truths, so understanding life does not require much effort. What makes life difficult is the inability to live by these truths, which you learn either from life itself or from those with experience.

I've read many books, written by wise people who have shared their wisdom on how to live and achieve success, which have inspired me. But there is nothing more fragile and unreliable than human nature. This was something that I did not always accept, blinded by my own will.

I was abducted on a Monday evening while returning home from work. Having left the university, I was walking along the street, when suddenly a van stopped next to me. Four big men jumped out, grabbed me, and tied my hands. They kicked and pushed me into the van and put a plastic bag over my head.

Because of my struggle and sudden fear, I remembered none of their faces. They hit me several times on the head, slammed me down on the floor between the seats, and stepped on me. I was like an animal caught in a trap in the forest. I shuddered and twitched, but in vain. Finally, the men must have gotten tired of my shaking and hit me so hard on the side of my head that I lost consciousness.

One of the thinkers I studied once said: "The most important and basic smell in a person is the smell of fear." I witnessed then how the emotions of desire, fear, and panic paralyzed my mind. I had never been so scared. We are not able to understand the extremes of someone else's personal tragedy as deeply as our own—its depth and dimensions.

More than the tragedy itself, it is the fear of other people's suffering that scares us. I used to feel like that. I ignored my neighbors, lived as if I had not seen their disasters, and fled from those who needed my help, as if from a contagious disease. But then, I myself endured disaster and ended up in a prison cell. It felt inevitable, like fate. I experienced shame, guilt, and rejection, all of these gradually, with the passing of each day, growing more intense until they finally became unbearably heavy. It is said that if one voluntarily accepts and confesses one's own guilt, the heart is freed from its heavy burden. That is why I confess my faults now, lying on a damp board in a narrow, dark cell of the underground prison. But no one hears my whispers, except for the stone wall.

I was even more worried for my mother than for myself: the fact that I disappeared must have completely shocked her. Poor thing—she had aged so quickly in recent years. I was the reason for it. My mother was deeply affected when I divorced my wife, my children going with her, and our house was left empty like a cemetery.

My mother worked hard all her life and sacrificed her age and health to raise me and my brothers. She endured relentless insults and humiliation from her relatives but clenched her teeth and made sure that her children were happy and their lives were in order. Nevertheless, I lost my way and let myself be deceived by the ease of youth and beauty. It was my mother who I betrayed first, not my wife. And now I am afraid that she will have a heart attack, that something bad will happen to her. Helpless, my soul cannot find its place either in my body or in this damp cell. To find peace, I immerse myself in memories.

I was ten or eleven years old when my family lived in a town not far from the Steppe District. My Aunt Gulizar lived in a small town near the seashore. When spring holidays came, I was sent to visit my aunt for two weeks. After the long voyage, the most awaited and exciting part began after I passed through the mountains: driving down the forest road that snaked its way up the steep slope, the sight of a shimmering sea on the horizon suddenly appeared for a few seconds, then disappeared among the trees. Dazzling green, blue, and white glimmers of light shone on the surface of the sea, and I felt a storm of excitement in my heart.

Every day, I went with Ibrahim, my uncle's son who was four years older than me, and his friend Osman to swim and walk along the coast. I liked the sea in the mornings and evenings most of all, when it was serene and gentle. I walked back and forth along the endless path, listening to Ibrahim's endless stories. As he talked, I looked among the pebbles brought to land by the sea waves for beautiful shells, colored glass, unusual stones, and lost jewelry. Someone once said that if you found a hollow stone, whispered your deepest wish to it, and threw it back into the sea, your wish would come true.

Some days, I found only four or five plain stones. I had one wish—to save my grandfather from a fatal illness that ruined the life of our family.

Ibrahim had about twenty rabbits. I loved these sweet animals so much that Ibrahim gave me two, a male and a female. At first, my father was not happy that I'd gotten the rabbits. All spring, I gathered grass and grapes in groves and orchards to feed them. Although my father helped me, I tried to clean the cages myself. Taking care of my rabbits brought me great joy and happiness. But one day, the female gave birth, then killed and ate several of her young. I felt as if I'd been doused with boiling water. The rest of the little rabbits grew up healthy, but after witnessing that, I felt a coldness towards rabbits that did not go away. Later, my father slaughtered them all.

Last year when he was not yet forty, Ibrahim died, after a lifetime of too much alcohol. He vomited blood for hours and was dead before morning, on the floor of his house that resembled an animal shed.

I can't tell you how much time I've spent in the cell here, because there are no windows and no light at all, except for a dirty, dim electric lamp that hangs from the ceiling. They light the lamp only when they give us food. They remove a cover at the bottom of the thick iron door and throw in a bowl with some slop, which is supposed to be food.

It is impossible to stand or sit or do anything except lie on this small plot of earth, only a few paces in width and length. Before I got used to this cell, the claustrophobia I experienced was insufferable. A lack of movement and the passing of time drove me mad. Sometimes I struggled to breathe; my head spun, my heart pounded, and I could find no escape from my suffering. I shouted again and again through the door, pleading with the guards not to turn the light off. Finally, when a light went on outside the door, two men in military uniforms entered with rubber sticks.

During the first days, nobody touched me. I was alone in this stone dungeon without light. I did not know if it was that the walls of the cell were so thick, or if I was completely alone in this prison. What I did know was that I could not hear the sound of anyone. I tried to laugh, to fill the overwhelming darkness with deafening joy. I sang songs and recited verses that I remembered. Sometimes, I repeated prayers from my childhood. When my voice began to sound hoarse, I realized that I would go crazy if I continued like that.

It was obvious that they wanted to break my will and destroy me. But, for some reason, as time passed, the fear in my soul subsided and I began to believe that this situation would somehow be good for me. So that hunger would not harm my body and mind, I ate their bad-smelling and bitter food. However, the intentions of my captors were not as I expected: they wanted to first give me hope, then take it away, by dragging me into the swamp of hopelessness and despair.

There are three essential elements to sanity. Pleasant memories show one the value of life and prove that it has not been wasted. Dreams of the future give one hope and strength to overcome obstacles; they inspire one to set goals and to continue to live. And finally, joy, which comes with food, safety, and creativity. The evil executioners who put me into prison cannot take possession of my memories and dreams. In the midst of my heartbreaking memories and dreams, my soul still remains with my body.

Once after shoving in a bowl of slop, they turned the light off, as usual, but soon turned it on again, as two soldiers entered the room and ordered me out of my cell. The feeling of fear that suddenly grabbed my throat made my stomach tighten and my knees tremble. I had to get up and follow the soldiers. They took me upstairs and I wondered if they were going to release me or kill me. Instead, they took me into a room where the impenetrable darkness of the night pressed against the windows and seemed about to invade the room.

A fat, stern-faced man at the head of the table began to interrogate me. At first, he threatened and insulted me, demanding that I confess to being an extremist who was leading a secret, anti-government organization. I denied this. Then, he and his partners began to beat me on the head, buttocks, back, stomach, and urged me to sign blank papers. When I refused, they gagged me, tied special wires to my naked body and genitals, and subjected me to electric shocks. Finally, I signed the papers.

But this would not be the end of it. The next time, they shoved a plastic tube emitting gas into my mouth. My eyes, nose, and throat burned and I vomited, struggling to breathe. They did not make any demands. They did this only to torture and humiliate me. I couldn't scream or resist anymore. My only wish was to die. To put an end to my bloody coughing, involuntary defecating, my headaches and body pain—this was all I wanted. After being tortured, lying on my knees in a dark, damp cell, shaking with exhaustion that consumed my body and soul, and breathing heavily with a wheezing sound in my lungs, I cursed my Creator, and my unfortunate fate, and prayed to Allah for death.

In this state of despair, I thought of the time I went to a funeral when the father of my classmate Sviatoslav died. It was one of those warm autumn days during the harvest when everyone ate grapes, apples, and pears. I was in the sixth grade, and our teacher suggested that we go to the funeral to console our classmate.

I was afraid of the red coffin, open in the middle of the courtyard, and the white-faced dead man inside it. This was the first time I'd seen a dead person. At the head of the coffin, swollen-eyed women in black scarves kissed the dead man, lamented over the body, and wept bitterly. As I watched, a well of horror opened in me, and my childish world plunged into the cold depths of that darkness. I experienced this same darkness once again when, as a first-year student, I attended the funeral of Yakup, who died in a car accident.

What is death, haunting us since the beginning of time and evoking an emotion as old as the universe? It is at once the simplest and most complex evidence of mortality, which is always before our eyes. From the point of view of existence, death is a very basic fact. But from the point of view of meaning and perception, death is inscrutable. A lifeless, motionless body lying in a tabut[3] is not an obvious truth. Those who witness it do not see it as natural. But this is only one side of the truth.

As I grew older, my attitude towards death mellowed, the fear receded, and sadness took its place. This was likely the result of education, experience, a set of different beliefs, growing older, learning to live with fear, and caring for others.

My deceased relatives, who were constantly coming to me in my dreams, made me somehow content and presented me with a kind of real peace. They almost erased the ravenous and foolish fear of death from my memory.

When the first victims of our tragedy appeared, there was no end to sadness and grief. People deceived themselves with mirth. But gradually, we grew anxious. The weight of poverty and age, which suddenly fell upon us, bent the shoulders and necks of many, wore down our stamina and resistance. Many of us got used to it, buried our heads in the sand, and pretended to deny what was obvious. It is true that this is an escape from action, shameful and disgraceful. The ultimate punishment for this is death.

I admit my guilt. When my fellow citizens needed help, I turned my back on them. It is my fault. I have no excuses and will not try to justify myself. An ordinary university teacher, I could have been declared an enemy. I could have lost my job, been forced to emigrate, or been imprisoned. These thoughts kept me tied hand and foot and from even secretly supporting the oppressed. But what I was most afraid of became reality. And, finally, I was taken by the hand and brought to this horrible, most dreadful place.

All of us will die somehow. The tyrant, the oppressed, the murderer and his victim, the hero and the refugee—everybody, sooner or later. We are absolutely and without a doubt doomed to disappear forever from the pages of history. A hundred or a hundred and fifty years later, no one will remember us. But I believe that after every death, there must surely be a resurrection. I believe that a person first grows up in the spirit world and then, finding an embryo, comes to life.

Secondly, when one leaves a mother's womb in agony, this kind of death leads to another birth. At the end of life, the soil, like a mother's womb, will receive the dead as a seed. But when the day of judgment comes, it will be rid of this heavy burden. Pain, vibrations, and loud sounds will wake the dead from a long sleep and they will once again have bodies. Those who have passed through the threshold of Berzah,[4] digging through the earth with their fingers in agony, struggling to get out on all fours, will come out of the groundwater and, completely naked, like newborns, re-enter the world.

I would like the cycle of life to go on like this, although I know it will probably never happen this way. My poor and unfortunate soul yearns for justice and revenge. These bloodsucking criminals must feel my severe suffering, the fear I felt when I thought I'd lost my mind, the physical and mental anguish that tore me to pieces. They must feel it fully, and then multiplied hundreds and thousands of times. This is my just revenge and natural right.

The dead people, whom I used to see in my dreams, are now standing behind me. I believe that they are waiting for me. Their sad, compassionate eyes and silence do not frighten me at all, now. I have somehow gotten used to them. Among them are my grandmother, Uncle Mamed, Yakup, Brother Ibrahim, Aunt Alie, Uncle Mirza, Aunt Safure, and so many others...

When my grandmother was alive, in her heart and memory, she held quiet conversations with her deceased relatives—her brothers and sisters, children, grandchildren, and others. During the day, closing herself in her room, she cried and moaned. Although I, too, tried to speak with the deceased in my dreams, not once did any of them answer me. They remained silent. They seemed to want to express their sad fates, but for some reason, I could not hear them. Their lips did not even move. Perhaps where they'd gone is too awful for words. If so, why didn't they scream instead? Was the longing in their eyes because of regret? I think so. It seems so. I also feel the anguish and regret now that fits awkwardly and painfully in my chest. Even if I opened up my soul and explained myself from beginning to end, I think that my guilt would not leave me. It would stay and continue to torment me.

To cope with lived regret, speaking out is essential. For a long time, I did not speak, did not say important words to my children or my spouse. Now I can only explain myself to cold, dull, harsh, dumb stones.

Forgive me, my children, I am so very sorry. I thought I was smart and quick-witted. I fooled myself, inventing thousands of deceitful words. I deceived you, too. And I realize that one cannot play with people's honor and fate. I don't know if this confession is repentance, advice, or prayer, but it is definitely not a complaint. I don't believe we'll see each other again. By falling into evil traps, I destroyed my identity, my consciousness, my hopes and dreams. I don't think that anybody will look for me and find me. The truth is that if a person is listed as missing, he will be completely forgotten. These simple truths are as clear as transparent amber stones, which by the power of imagination and perception will take the form of enchanted beads, making possible a transformation. Honed and processed, perception will pass through the thread of the soul and turn into a spiritual rosary, a personification of graceful wisdom. The one who touches such a rosary will acquire the power of touching his life and controlling it by his own will. This is a work of art you cannot touch with your hand or see with your eye. It is perceived only by the soul and is known by the light of a person's eyes. But not everyone is destined to see this.

I know that the stone walls of my cell are listening to me because everything has its own soul. If not, why should people turn their faces to the thick and ancient walls, buildings, and dwellings of their country, and whisper their most secret dreams and desires?

Is it possible that this river of dreams and longings, flowing continuously since time immemorial, will be in vain? Stones listen and record everything in their memory. If someone who understands their language asks them delicately about something, the stones will not hesitate to respond.

I lie on my side on the floor of a dark and damp prison cell. Delirious, I share my thoughts and feelings about my predicament with the black walls. Because only they can hear me whisper and because suffering consumes my soul and body, I lose consciousness. Then I come to my senses. Trembling, shaking, groaning, I wholeheartedly open my eyes and wait for the last breath. Now, I do not curse Allah. I do not curse my misfortune. I do not blame myself, either. I know that this blind prison will be my witness.

1   Zindan—a prison built deep in the ground
2   Tata—sister
3   Tabut—coffin
4   Berzah—an intermediate state or place between death and resurrection

My Blue-Eyed Adile

Zekiye Ismailova

Adapted by David R. Earl
and Scott Aumont

"Adile! Adile-ee!"

Hearing her name, the old woman woke from her reverie and looked around. The other passengers on the train car were reading newspapers, talking, eating, or just settling in.

"Adile!"

A group of young people on the platform had come up to the window and knocked on the glass.

"I'm here!"

A pretty young girl leaned over her to wave to her friends.

"Goodbye, see you!" she shouted before noticing the vacant seat next to the old woman.

She turned to her.

"Is this seat free? May I sit?"

"Certainly. Sit, my dear," the old woman said, looking carefully at the girl. She was thin and seemed gentle, her sky-blue eyes full of joy and laughter; when she smiled, dimples appeared on her cheeks. Her blond hair hung down to her waist, and she was wearing a blue dress that matched the color of her eyes. *What a good girl, well-mannered and polite,* the old woman thought to herself. *Let Allah bless you and open the way to your happiness. Let those of our people in Crimea grow and live there happily.*

Do our people, who survived so much pain and horror, finally have the right to live freely in their homeland? she wondered.

The girl reminded her of her own youth. She'd been thirteen when the war began. After the enemy invaded and fighting started in Crimea, her father, who worked on the railway, gathered the family and took them to a place away from the roads and the city center—a place at the foot of Mount Mangup, where the enemy was unlikely to attack. But rural life was very different from the noisy city. Its empty spaces were filled with silence, a stillness so complete that Adile became bored. Moving to the city, she'd lost contact with most of her old friends.

After telling the village children where she'd come from and what she'd learned in the city, she divided them into squads; she marched them from the lower to the upper quarter of the village; they climbed the pine trees and played hide-and-seek.

Adile had a little brother, but he was small, so she became her father's main assistant. Going with him to the chaiyir[1] was Adile's greatest pleasure. On their way, he told her stories, recalling his own childhood. She loved helping him with the grafts. She also liked herding a cow on Mount Mangup. While the grass in the valley had yellowed, it remained green on the hill. All the children brought the cattle there to graze—though most of the herders were boys.

Adile's older, married sister lived with them, but she was pregnant, so she stayed home helping her mother with the housework and taking care of her brothers and sisters. Her sister's husband, meanwhile, was at the front. Adile's father was too old to be drafted. He worked plowing the meadow and planting grain. Adile helped with the ox. The animal would usually walk on its own, but when it stopped, it had to be pulled.

After the cow was milked, her mother made her breakfast—a slice of pita and a piece of cheese. Afterwards, she let the cow out of the barn. Adile, by herself, drove the animal alongside the other children along the road to the top of Mangup. Summer days passed quickly; in the fall there was school. No one had imagined that the war would be so hard, bloody, and tragic. The newsreels kept promising that victory would come soon.

In school, Adile refused to be bullied by the boys. Not even her neighbor Khalil, the biggest of the lot, wanted to mess with her after she once knocked him down and began smacking him on the head with a book. The teachers finally had to separate them.

By the autumn of 1943, the war had already been going on for three years. After the collapse of Akyar[2] and the defeat on the Kerch peninsula, all of Crimea fell into the hands of the enemy. With the Soviet troops pushed out of Crimea, the school closed. The Germans maintained their presence through a designated local collaborator.

But life in the village went on. The children continued to play and perform their chores.

And Adile again found herself having to fight. This time, Yakub and Mustafa, two boys from the neighboring region, approached when she was gathering grass.

Adile immediately confronted them.

"What are you doing here?" she said, beating Yakub with her fists.

Mustafa ran to help her. Then Khalil jumped in, followed by Sabri, then Khadija, then Shefika, then Ilyas. Adile's younger sister Jevair, along with her brother Jafer, also joined in the mayhem... and the whole melee of children could hardly be separated.

"A girl shouldn't behave like that," the adults who witnessed the brawl agreed. But when they tried telling Adile how girls should act, she snapped back:

"You mean it's ok that these guys take over my turf? And if one of them pulls my hair, I should smile and say thank you?"

She glared at Khalil and shook her fist.

"Yakub and Mustafa have already got what they deserved. And you will too," she said, still furious.

"I didn't even touch you," he said.

"Sabri saw you pulling my hair," she insisted, promising to show him where the crayfish hibernate.[3]

Khalil laughed and teased her:

"A girl goat's no different from a boy goat," he said, a folk teaser that meant girls were as ill-mannered and shameless as boys.

The children who were watching joined in the taunting:

"A boy goat, a girl goat, a boy goat, a girl goat!"

Adile blushed. "You just wait, I'll show you," she said, already plotting revenge.

Not here, not now… can't go to their homes… Best wait till we're where the cows graze.

She imagined herself leaping out of the bushes, throwing herself at him, kicking him into the dust.

She calmed down, threw back her tangled, fluffy hair, braided it again, and laughing, shook her fist at the boys who teased her as she shouted:

"Let Allah take all his problems! Just remember I'm watching you."

"The knife is propped on the bone. I'll get you for this," Adile continued, scolding Khalil, still plotting her revenge.

It wouldn't be easy; Khalil was no wimp. His father was a blacksmith, a strong man, and Khalil was tall and broad-shouldered, like his father. His hands had been forged in the smithy alongside his old man, crushing iron with a hammer.

She might not beat him in direct combat, but there were other ways…

On the way home, she continued plotting. Seeing Yaya aga's[4] fence, she had an idea.

"I've got it!" she exclaimed.

Adile woke early the next morning. *She had to get there before Khalil.*

"Mom, did you milk the cow? I'm ready to go," she announced, slipping pita and cheese into her bag.

"Allah-Allah, my child, what's the sudden rush?" her mother asked.

Adile wasn't often out of bed early. Her mother usually had to prod her awake.

"Nothing," Adile shrugged. "I heard what you said yesterday and I'm trying to be polite, nice, well-mannered. I am trying to obey you. Am I doing it wrong, mom?" she answered in a low voice, looking at her mother innocently. Surprised, not knowing what to say, her mother let the girl pass out the door.

"She actually listened to my words?" she pondered. *"That's so unlike Adile. Must be a reason. But what?"*

The cow ambled along the familiar path while Adile raced ahead to Yaya aga's fence. She climbed it and lay still.

Khalil, bag on his back, rod in hand, walked along the road whistling a tune. A big black cow stepped ahead of the other cattle.

Adile lay sprawled along the top of the fence, waiting. As soon as the boy passed by, she jumped. Caught by surprise, Khalil tumbled into the puddle.

Sitting on his back, Adile screeched: "Had enough? Have a little more!"

And she pounded her fists on the head and shoulders of the boy she hated. "I'll show you! *A boy goat, a girl goat...*"

The boy recovered and rose, shaking her off easily.

Wiping the mud from his face, he looked at her without anger:

"Well, haven't you done just what I said you would do? Who are you now, Adile?" he asked.

Dumbstruck, Adile stared intently into the boy's face. From under thick dark eyebrows, smiling brown eyes looked at her. Despite the fact he was covered in mud, Khalil remained dignified and unbowed.

Shrugging, he said: "So, this is all you are." Then he turned and went home to change his clothes.

She'd expected he would beat her, knock her into the mud, or at least scold and shame her, but nothing like that happened.

Surprised, maybe even ashamed, she screamed:

"Hey, why did you turn your back and leave? You afraid to fight me?!"

The boy didn't bother looking back.

"Coward! Coward!" she screamed.

Finally, he turned: "I don't fight girls," he simply said, and walked on.

His heart sank. Why, why couldn't he say anything more to this girl? When looking into her sky-blue eyes, he went dumb.

What did he mean, she wondered. Adile remembered Khalil's face. The eyes, which had once seemed so cold, had looked at her with a warmth that couldn't help touching her heart. She was suddenly filled with emotions that she had never experienced before. What was going on? Unable to find the answer, she dusted herself off and slowly went on her way. She found Khalil's black cow in the herd and drove her to the pasture.

But Khalil wasn't there.

At home, Adile wondered what had happened. Had she offended him? Had she overdone it? She suddenly saw herself as she might have looked from the outside. Always playful and laughing, Adile now fell silent and withdrew into herself. Emotions she had never felt in her heart before, thoughts that had never crossed her mind, upset her. Not understanding what was happening, she decided to admit her mistake and apologize.

"Is everything all right, child? Are you feeling okay?" Her mother's voice interrupted her reverie.

"No, no, nothing's wrong. I am just..."

Then Adile suddenly imagined taking the cow to graze again and meeting Khalil at the fence. She feared she wouldn't even be able to look at the boy.

"I seem to have caught a little cold. Can't my older sister take out the cow to graze tomorrow?"

"Of course not, she is pregnant. Her stomach is practically touching her nose. How will she climb the mountain behind the cow? Now, open your mouth, let me see," Adile's mother said, looking at the back of her throat for signs of a cold. "No, there's nothing."

"What about my younger brother and sister? Why do I always have to do this? Let them take the cow up the mountain for once," the girl insisted.

"Something's definitely wrong, something's happened! You usually can't wait to get out there."

Realizing this wouldn't trick her mother, Adile tried to get pity instead.

"Oh, mom, they tease me! *'A boy goat, a girl goat,'* I'm already so tired, I don't want to go anymore—I won't go. Let the cow sit in the stall; I'll pick her grass in the valley..."

Angry, her mother propped her chin on her hand, looking at her daughter attentively. Then she shook her head.

"When your father arrives, you yourself will answer," she said, and turned to the side of the table to continue kneading dough.

"We would also go with you to pick grass," Adile's little brother and sister said, just now entering the room, having heard her last words. They hugged her around her neck. She calmed down, and sighed deeply. She knew she would eventually have to meet Khalil face-to-face and apologize. When her father entered the house, Adile had made up her mind.

"Wake me up early in the morning," she said and went to bed.

Well, what's the problem? she said to herself. *If I have to see him, I'll see him... Aren't we neighbors? Even when just going out the door, I could meet him.*

She repeated again and again to herself what she would do and what she would tell him when they inevitably met.

Khalil was panicked. Struggling within him was the flame of anger mingled with a feeling he could not define. One thing he knew very well: he could never cause the slightest harm to this girl. As soon as they moved to this village, he always noticed Adile without knowing why. On the first day, she came up to their fence and said, "Hello, I am Adile, your neighbor." She looked at him and he was enchanted by her large, blue eyes. "What is your name?" she said, at once stealing away his heart and mind.

He would watch her eruptions of temper, not interfering in anything; he didn't dare approach her. And having lived for three years with this suffering, the boy for the first time did not know what to do.

Coward—the word thrown after him—set him on fire, knocked him down. *What should I do to prove otherwise? How to get this girl's attention?* His friends looked askance at him because he did not allow anybody to say a single bad word about Adile. Recently, when his best friend Midat asked him if he had fallen in love with this girl, he got it good from him. Later, Khalil apologized, but Midat did not forgive him. Now, they didn't get along at all.

Ah, Adile, what have you done with me? thought the suffering teenage boy. Well, Khalil thought, he didn't even think it was love, until Midat asked his question. There was no one with whom he could share the secret; there was no one to whom he could open his soul. How to explain what he was feeling when he also didn't know? He had no idea what to do. It was enough for him to see her from afar. Let her be there, whatever she says, let her only say—

But of course, I'm a coward. I'm afraid of expressing my feelings, to confess to her. If I tell her I love her, she will destroy me with her laughter.

That's her nature. And I love her for it. The war is everywhere, people are dying. The enemy is everywhere, and you think about love?

He was ashamed of his thoughts.

War… Maybe I'll become a volunteer and run away to the front? I am sixteen years old, but I could say seventeen… or eighteen… I can easily add some years…

He imagined himself wounded, receiving medals, becoming a hero, returning home from the war, and that Adile came out to meet him…

Nonsense!—Khalil suddenly stopped himself.

Crimea is in the hands of the invaders. Where will you go as a volunteer? If you go out of the village, they immediately say that you are a migrant worker and then take you away… May Allah protect me.

But I can contact the partisans. My uncle is with them. If I go to my aunt and tell her that I want to join my uncle, she won't say no. My father and my brother are at the front.

I've decided—it's time to put away childish things.

But what will my mother say? he suddenly wondered.

He was sure it would be hard to convince her, but he would be firm in his decision and stand his ground. He would go and join the partisans until the Germans went away, his mother wouldn't say anything about it. She was terrified that the Germans would take her son to Germany. Not so long ago, Mustafa, the headman of the village, warned the people: "Take care that the teenagers do not go outside!"

The problem at home was solved.

But how to tell Adile? Should I say it on the pasture while casually passing by her? "Oh, you won't see me anymore, I'm going to war."

Or, "By the way, I'm going to the front…"

But would she listen to me at all? What if she accuses me of cowardice again? I could simply tell her: "It's okay, I'm not a coward, calm down, you'll soon be rid of me, I'm going to the front…"

In a month, the forest warden Abduraman aga is going to leave for Yalta on business. I will join him and go to my uncle. My mother will not be visiting him again.

After making his decision, Khalil relaxed, breathing a sigh of relief. In bed, he fantasized again that he returned home as a hero, imagined those who came out to meet him, and finally fell asleep. These were youthful dreams.

The night turned cold, and snow covered the ground. The children, dressed in warm clothes, drove the cows up the hill. Khalil looked around and did not see Adile. His heart sank. Had she not come out, or did she come out early and he failed to see her?

"Shoo!" he said, hastening the animal, hitting it lightly with a rod. He started his climb, and soon on the edge of a cliff saw several children standing, bewildered.

"What's going on? Why are you gathered there? Get away; you could fall there!" Khalil shouted.

"Aga! Our sister, Adile has fallen," one of them said.

"What?! Adile?" He felt sick inside. "Adile!!" he shouted and ran to the edge of the abyss. As it was explained to him, little Zinep's foot had slipped by the edge, and she nearly fell over. Adile saw her and pulled Zinep aside, but then she slipped herself and fell into the abyss. Luckily, at the last moment, she managed to catch on to the roots of a bush.

Khalil saw her. She was one or two meters from the edge of the cliff, but too far to reach by hand. A rope was needed.

"Guys! Who has a long thick rope?" Khalil asked. At once, several hands passed him ropes attached to the necks of animals. Khalil wanted to throw one end of the rope to Adile and pull her out. However, she had been hanging in this position for a long time and her hands became stiff; he realized also that she was exhausted. It was impossible.

"Adile, how are you? Wait, I'll... Look, I'll tie a rope. You'll put it over your head and under your arms. You are a strong, brave girl! Don't be afraid, I'll pull you out... Do you understand?"

"I understand," Adile answered in a tired voice. Hearing this voice, Khalil's heart sank. He tied the rope, measured its length, and, laying down on the edge of the cliff, threw the rope down to her. At first, Adile carefully released one hand, put the rope over her head and under one arm, then under the other.

Khalil watched and asked, "Are you ready?" When Adile nodded, he began to pull. From the adrenaline, he did not even feel the weight of the girl. He noted that she was light, very light, like a bird. The girl's head cleared the edge; she stretched out her hands and seized the hands of Khalil. He let go of the rope, taking her by the armpits and pulling her towards him. They hugged for a while and looked into each other's eyes. Now the girl understood what trouble she had escaped from. If Khalil had come too late, her hands would not have been able to endure, her hands would have weakened…

For a long time, recovering themselves, they lay silent on the edge of the cliff, looking at the sky. *Exactly like the Crimean sky*, he thought when he saw Adile's eyes, pulling her upward.

"Thank you for saving me," she said, turning her head towards Khalil.

"My pleasure. No need to thank me, you would have done the same…" he said, confused. "Come on, get up, the ground is cold now," he said, jumping up lightly, and offering his hand to Adile to help her. The children took a deep breath and dispersed.

"You can let go of my hands now," she said smiling. Only then did Khalil realize he was still squeezing her hands. He was embarrassed and suddenly let go, and fell silent, not knowing what to say. He stepped aside.

"Will you forgive me for what I said?" asked Adile, earnestly.

"I have forgotten a long time ago and I didn't take any offense."

"Okay, but I wasn't fair. Can we bury the hatchet?" she said, her blue eyes staring into his.

"Peace," Khalil said not taking his eyes off the girl's face, as if he wanted to keep her there in his memory forever.

"Why are you staring at me like that?" she asked sharply, coming to herself.

"No, it's just that…" the boy grew confused. "I will go to Yalta in a week…"

"Why? Will you be there for a long time?" Adile asked.

"No, just a few things to do, then I'll be back," he said, avoiding the details. "Well, I have only one week left. If you want, we can walk up together this week…"

"As if we have alternative ways to go," she answered, laughing, turning the conversation into a joke to hide her anxiety and excitement.

The week flew by in the blink of an eye. Every day, the two walked together, spent their time chatting, gathered with the children and played hide-and-seek. On their last evening, Khalil called Adile to the door and said: "I'm leaving tonight."

"I know," she said coquettishly. She understood that he'd singled her out from the other girls.

"Reach out and open your hand."

She obliged. The boy placed a copper ring that he had made himself into her hand. The ring had patterns of leaves carved into it.

"It's wonderful, did you make it yourself?"

"I don't know for sure when I'll be back. Actually, I want to join the partisans... I want you to remember me by this ring..."

"No! How did this happen? Why? If you are killed..!" Tears flashed in her eyes.

"Don't worry, I'll be back when we drive the enemy out of Crimea. Keep the ring. Look, I have the same one." The boy showed a sparkling ring on his finger. "When I return, I will make you a gold ring. Will you wait for me?"

They did not know that this was their last meeting. What can you say? It's youth. At the time, you think everything goes easily, quickly. Crimea was, in fact, liberated from the enemy, but then came exile... All the people were devastated.

No matter how much she searched for him, Adile could not find even a trace of Khalil. She heard that while he was with the partisans, he was wounded, but she couldn't find out where he'd gone.

In the end, many years passed; she got married and had a family, and was fortunate to return to her homeland, to Crimea, but this unanswered question in her heart grew stronger every time she remembered. Perhaps, if she knew the fate of Khalil, she would not feel so bad, so upset...

"Granny, granny! Are you alright? Do you need medicine, water, or something else?" The girl, who had gotten into the train car and taken a seat next to her, kindly and carefully took the old woman by the hand and looked into her eyes.

"I'm fine, child. It's old age. My blood pressure dropped, perhaps."

"Oh, what a ring you have!" the girl pointed to the ring on the old woman's little finger. "This is something from the old days, isn't it?"

"It is so, my child. It is a memory of my life when the war started."

"I've seen a ring with the same pattern somewhere, but I don't remember… Wait, of course! I saw it in the box where my grandfather's medals were… only it was black, probably made of copper…"

"Mine is also copper, but my son tinned it so that it would not turn black," she carefully looked at the girl's face and asked: "Who is your grandfather, what is his name?"

"My grandfather's name is Khalil, but he died; I was ten years old when he passed away. We lived in Saratov[5] at first, then we moved to Kherson,[6] but he could never return to Crimea. He wanted to see his village. The village doesn't exist anymore. I remember he always asked his fellow villagers and his relatives about a girl named Adile. He named me after her, you know. I look like my mother, but he was very happy that I had such blue eyes and blond hair."

The old woman studied her face attentively.

"And who are you? Did you know my grandfather?" asked the girl.

The old woman nodded her head:

"I am Adile, we are namesakes," she said.

He didn't die, he was saved, he lived his life, glory to Allah, the old woman thought and said.

"Alla dzhanyny rahmet eilesin, yatkan eri jennet olsun,"[7] she said, wiping away tears with the end of the kerchief on her head.

"Wait, are you Adile, the one my grandfather was looking for?" the girl looked even closer at the face of the old woman. "Of course, you are! As my grandfather told me, the eyes are light blue… And the ring…"

The girl got up in excitement and sat down next to the old woman. She kissed her hand and stroked it, then hugged the old woman. "It's as if I saw my grandfather. He loved me very much. He talked a lot about the old Crimean life."

No matter how a person changes, the eyes remain the same. Adile's eyes were as blue as in her youth.

My blue-eyed Adile, the old woman remembered Khalil's words, as if it were a greeting from the past.

The train stopped at Aqmescit.[8] People rushed through the station like millet. The girl helped the old woman up, taking her luggage, and stepped off the train.

"Adile, Adileshka! I'm here," said a tall, strong young man waving and approaching them with a smile.

"Excuse me, do we know each other? I can't remember you. How do you know my name?"

The young man said with a smile and held out his hand: "It's nice to meet you. Seeing as we don't know each other, let's get acquainted. I'm Khalil."

The sight of this beautiful girl did not leave him indifferent. Taken aback, the girl looked around. The old woman stepped aside and took the young man under his arm. She looked at the girl and said:

"My dear, meet my grandson Khalil. As a child he called me by that name, and it has remained this way…"

1   Chaiyir—a garden in the forest where Crimean Tatars used to graft trees
2   Akyar—the Crimean Tatar name for Sevastopol, a city in the southwest of the Crimean peninsula
3   To show where the crayfish hibernate—to teach someone a lesson
4   "Aga" is used to express respect or recognition.
5   Saratov, a city in Russia
6   Kherson, a city in Ukraine
7   "Alla dzhanyny rahmet eilesin, yatkan eri jennet olsun"—"May the Lord bless his soul, may his resting place be in heaven."
8   Aqmescit—the Crimean Tatar name of Simferopol, the second-largest city on the Crimean Peninsula

This is Just What You Need!

Zekiye Ismailova

Adapted by Shubha Sunder
and Scott Aumont

Eyes closed, the young man groped for the phone on the table beside him.

"I'm listening," he said.

"Honey, I need to go to the nail salon. Our friends have a wedding party tomorrow, remember? We're invited, and I have to be the most beautiful, right? I wanted to tell you earlier, I made an appointment for nine o'clock. You know how bad the traffic is then."

Breaking into his sweet dream, the thin, gentle voice that used to please him now only made him nervous. How are you doing, how do you feel—no such words now, not even a greeting. Instead, straight to business, and what is it?

That's enough. I'm done being her chauffeur... I spent the whole day yesterday driving from one store to another to do her business. I put my own work on hold and stayed up all night repairing a car for a customer. It was morning when I finally went to bed. No. Too much pressure. If it continues like this... No, impossible.

"Call a taxi," he said politely, masking his anger. "I'm still sleeping. I set aside all my work yesterday to drive you around so you could find a dress. I'd just fallen asleep when you woke me up. I'm very tired. Barely conscious. I'm sorry, I can't go on the road like this."

"Well, Osik, that won't work. I've been counting on you to take me. My appointment is at nine o'clock. There was no other time and the rest of the slots were already taken. I absolutely need to paint my nails. You remember I showed you how the paint on my left index finger is peeling off. It needs to be refreshed. Before a taxi arrives—"

She hesitated. "If you don't come, I'll never speak to you again, and I'll go to the wedding with Anafi."

"Do what you want." He could barely stand the girl's chatter and was ready to throw the phone across the room.

"Is that your last word?"

Osman shuddered at the sudden chill in that thin, gentle voice.

I've always put up with her coquetry. The one time I say no, she kicks me out? What happens in the end, I wonder? I don't even want to think about it.

"The last," he said, and hung up.

So, now there's also this Anafi. She's been fooling another one too. What a sucker I am for not suspecting anything. This girl—wherever we went, I could feel everyone's eyes on her. It made me proud that such a beautiful girl was with me. And now I see the other side. I wonder, which of us is the "fallback," me or Anafi?

Pulling the covers over his head, Osman remembered the days when he was first getting to know Sebile. How he worried she would reject him—the very thought was paralyzing. He was never quite sure how to take what she said. After handing her a bouquet of flowers on their first date, she'd suggested he might also have brought a few boxes of chocolates and he took it as a joke. He should have stayed cool, but he was so in love, there were many things he didn't notice. He even boasted to his grandmother, with whom he always shared his secrets. Studying her photo, his grandmother said that the girl was beautiful but looked very flirtatious. *Didn't you always tell me it was okay for a girl to flirt a little,* he'd asked. *What can I say, think about it yourself,* she'd replied gnomically.

He assumed that his grandmother did not approve of his girlfriend but, to Osman, Sebile was the most beautiful, noble, and angelic girl in the world. Eventually, though, Sebile's whims began to weary him.

And this was the last straw. Newly liberated, he took a deep breath. He had no regrets. Now he could do as he liked, he was free. Osman went back to sleep.

"Hey, what's up? It's noon and you're still sleeping."

He woke to his good friend and colleague shaking him by the shoulder.

"Aaah, Luman, hey, brother." He sat up, and they shook hands. "Did you deliver the car to the client?"

"Of course. He asked about you. I told him you were busy repairing a car somewhere else. He was delighted and asked me to thank you, but I said what would really make a difference is if he shared our business cards with his friends."

"Great job! That car really pissed me off. I'm so tired."

"I thought fixing it was child's play for you. You should have told me."

"You were at your other job, and besides, I was with Sebile all day long, and I didn't get to start work on the car until late. I didn't want to bother you. Hey, go into the kitchen. My grandmother seems to be making pancakes. Do you smell that? Let me just wash up."

The young man picked up his clothes and went to the bathroom.

"Come in, my son, take a seat, I'll pour you some tea," said the thin, smiling old woman to Luman. "Or would you prefer coffee?"

"Thank you, Aunt Urmus," he said, kissing the old woman's hand.[1] "How are you? How's your health?"

"What can you say? At my age... I try to keep working. If I don't move, my knees get stiff and then I can't even walk."

"What do the doctors say?"

"Who goes to the doctor? And if I do go, what can he do? As if anyone knows anything these days."

"He might prescribe some kind of ointment. Some medications."

"Oh, there is no cure for old age. If I could see you married. With children," she said, looking at Osman, "my soul would be at peace, and I wouldn't worry so much about dying."

"Oh, grandmother, don't talk nonsense, don't worry about your soul," said Osman entering the room, with the smell of fresh soap and water following him. "And who will dance the haitarma[2] at my wedding party and tell fairy tales to my children?"

"I am always telling you, get married, get married. My tongue and throat are drying up, but you don't care. Where is this girl? What was her name, Seville?"

"Sebile. It's all over, grandmother, there is no 'this girl' anymore."

"What are you talking about? Did something happen?"

"She's no longer in my life." He explained the situation quickly, trying to calm the old woman's nerves. "I feel sick, honestly. O Allah, do not ask me anything. But I'm glad our relationship ended. What jam do you like with your pancakes, granny?" Osman said, trying to change the topic.

"Your favorite tea rose jam. I don't even know what to say. Should I cry or should I be happy?"

"You should be happy, grandmother. I'm glad I was spared. Are there no other girls left in our district? If things do not work out with one girl, we'll find another, right?"

"You know yourself... Yes, please, explain..."

"Don't spoil my appetite. Let's enjoy our meal. What job do we have for today?" he asked Luman, eager to shift the conversation to his work-related problems. "Did they bring us the spare parts we ordered?"

"Yes," Luman said. "Timur brought them yesterday. Let's call that guy and let him know the parts for his car have arrived. By the time he gets here, our work will be done. Refat is in the workshop right now. He'll let us know if something happens."

"If that's the case, we have a little time to sit. Let's go into my room. I have a few ideas I want to run by you."

They'd begun as locksmiths at the same service station. Smart and diligent, they learned the basics and then opened their own garage where they'd been working together for several years. Word spread about the high quality of their work and soon the business was generating excellent returns. The two young men began dressing better. They bought new cars and generally managed to enjoy themselves. Their houses were built on the plots of land their parents had managed to buy years earlier. Everything seemed to be going well. But in this country there is always a 'but.' The future was never stable. Still, life goes on...

"So what happened? Why did you break up with Sebile?"

"Nothing to explain. I'm just fed up." The young man drew his finger across his throat. "Lately I've done nothing but cater to her whims. *I want this, I want that, take me there, take me here...* I'm sick of it. I spent all yesterday driving her around town on errands. I couldn't get to my own work until after dinner and then she called me at dawn and asked me to come and pick her up because she needed to get a manicure, can you believe it!? It's over. And another thing... What's the name of that guy..? Fikret? Anyway, she said that if I didn't come, she would call *him* instead!"

"So this other dude is already on the line for her?" said Luman. "Well, Lenara and I seem to be on the verge of breaking up. She's also starting to annoy me. I give her small gifts when I can. She asked for a ring, I gave her a ring. She asked for a dress, I bought it. Now she wants the latest iPhone... You know, I'm not stingy, but we're not even engaged. Thank God. Maybe she also has a Fikret. These girls must think we're donkeys."

"Don't say that, my friend."

"Look, Instagram is full of beautiful girls. No need to rush things. We can pick and choose and have a little fun along the way." Luman started flipping through his cell phone. "What about this one?" He pulled up a photo of a girl.

"Hard to say. How do you know if that's her or if she posting someone else's photo?"

"Just take a look first."

"Nothing special about her, quite passable..."

"Well, let's click and take a closer look... Oh, no, there's a young man standing nearby, they may be dating... Here's another beauty..."

"In my opinion, she looks a little artificial, pouting her lips, maybe..."

"Maybe so, but she looks like a doll!"

"No, I'm tired of such dolls. I need a simple, ordinary girl, no makeup, no tricks..."

Swiping, Luman found another. "Look at this one. The eyes and eyebrows are all in place, and the makeup is barely visible. And the name is good. *Ayshe.* Grandma would love her."

"Do you look for a girl for your grandmother?" Osman asked. "If there's no makeup, who knows how many filters and photoshops this picture went through..."

"You're right! I once fell for this type of thing. The photo was flawless. In reality her face was pockmarked and full of pimples. You can pity the poor thing, but I was not ready for that at all."

"Happened to me once, too. A beautiful girl, no question, but the girl in the photo was pale as milk, and the one I met in person had a much darker complexion… Why such tricks? If you love someone, you'll love her acne and her color, but when you're meeting for the first time and a completely different person from the one in the photo shows up…"

The young men fell into silence, staring at their phones. Eventually, Osman said to his friend, "I don't know, it seems I liked this Ayshe you mentioned. Should I ping her? Let's see if she answers…"

"Go ahead. By the way, do you remember that ginger-haired Ibrahim?"

"Yes, what about him?"

"Married."

"Really? Why didn't he say anything?"

"He messed up with Marushke.[3] He used to be with a nice girl. Then that Marushke got between them. What she did, how she did it, I don't know, but in the end, she married him. His parents were upset and angry. They didn't even arrange a wedding party. Instead, they rented a house and settled them there."

"Well, what a donkey. Complete jerk."

"Just what I'm saying. And now, if this Marushke says "Get up," he gets up. She says, "Sit down," he sits down. She has him wrapped around her little finger. Boy, I wouldn't even be surprised to hear that she has him doing the laundry."

Ayshe returned home from the university in a bad mood. She'd almost been hit on the ring road by a car zooming across the lanes. She'd noticed just in time and managed to swerve to the side. Lately, everyone, even Ayder, was making her nervous. They'd just met and were only starting to get to know each other. Still, he'd helped himself to her cell phone and asked her things like, "Why is this young man writing to you? Who is he? Delete your photo, upload a cat or a flower or something else for an avatar. Who's this? What's his business? He's just sent you a message."

"It's my own business," she shot back. "I don't like it if someone has a cat or a car instead of a photograph. I have no secrets. If you look at someone's photo, it's clear at once who you're talking to, and if you don't like them, you can say no..."

The girl entered the house. She was greeted by silence. Her parents were still at work. There was food in the fridge, the rooms were clean. No one around to make a mess. Ayshe warmed up her food, ate it, and went to her room. She needed to finish her coursework. It didn't take her long. And now she had time to spare. Mavile had suggested they go to Meganom[4] together to have some fun. Ayshe decided to call and ask her.

The number was busy. Ayshe smiled. It was clear Mavile was gossiping again. She'd answer when she finished her conversation.

Oh, that Mavile. It was always who meets who? When? What does he do? Where does he live? She knew everything about everybody. Thinking about Mavile cheered Ayshe up. She had the energy of ten people. She managed work, study, and house chores all at once. She was always gentle, sweet, and cheerful... And she didn't like Ayder either. His family was arrogant and haughty. She heard people saying that they were looking for a bride with a degree, who could drive a car, make good money, and with rich and/or famous parents. Did they think they were buying cattle at the market, or what? What about feelings, emotions? Or did they just want money?

Ayshe remembered a cousin who'd been in love with a girl, spent all his salary on her. They looked like they belonged together. But, either because he was from a middle-class family, or because he was simple and open, or because she didn't fancy the car he drove, she rejected her cousin and married another, richer one. Recently, she'd seen this girl with her husband at a wedding party. Sitting side-by-side, they sure didn't look like newlyweds, with no signs of affection between them. Each was gazing in a different direction...

Bored, Ayshe started flipping through her phone. Ah, here was the message that had offended Ayder.

"Hello. How are you?"

What do you care? She shrugged. *I wonder who it is... Ah, well, here's a photo. He looks good, I don't know what to write... Okay, if he's really serious, he'll write again.*

Meanwhile, the phone rang. Mavile...

Osman was in Kyiv on business. The weather was cool and, after walking around the city a little, he felt cold and returned to his rented room. Bored, he turned on the TV. Talk, talk talk... Just empty chatter... The telephone rang.

"Luman, right on time! I'm just hanging out. Things are okay. How about you? Good? We've got several orders and the spare parts are here, but how to get them across the border?"

After discussing a few contracts and other business, he said, "Goodbye, say hello to your family," and hung up.

Silence again. He began scrolling through pages on his cell phone. Several unanswered messages from Sebile.

I think I'd better block her. Let her find someone else. Let me check out Ayshe again. She hasn't answered yet. She's stubborn. Maybe she's already seeing someone. I wrote her out of the blue... Oh, no, it's nothing like that! Now, who's this? They're sitting side by side. What a great smile... The boy's not bad-looking. Looks like a Turkish actor with a neat beard. Ah, her brother... What's wrong with me?

He opened the cell phone's camera and looked at himself. Over the last few days his beard had grown.

I'm no worse than her brother... Should I write again or what? What should I write? What if I tell her I'm in Kyiv and can bring her whatever she might need? Why not? It would give us a reason to meet...

Osman did just that.

Ah, she's typing a response!

—if it's not too difficult for you, Citramon,[5] please, for my mother, she wrote.

—and for you?

—for me, if it is not too much... Sorry, it's hard to ask a complete stranger...

—don't worry, ask. Tomorrow I'll be in Simferopol, God willing...

—if so, then for me, a little something that all the girls want, a little something in a red wrapper...

This worried him. The cell phone slipped from his hands and fell to the ground. *Here you go... could that happen, I wonder? Should*

I go to a store and buy her something made especially for women?? The ginger-haired Ibrahim came to his mind at once. Got what you deserved. Do not laugh at your neighbor; it will come back to bite you, isn't that what they say? Even so, no one dragged you by the tongue. You made a promise, now you can't take it back. It's good no one you know is around, no one will see you. Don't tell Luman; he'll die laughing. What does this girl want, I wonder?

He picked up his cell phone and continued reading.

—it doesn't matter if it is "Korona," "Svitoch," or "Roshen." [6] *There's also the kind with hazelnuts, but can you find and buy it? Do you have enough money?*

Eh, thank Allah, it's not what he thought! Just chocolate. Osman relaxed. Mixed emotions washed over him: calm, surprise, and delight. *I'm such a nervous Nelly,* he thought.

—with pleasure, my dear, he wrote. *As much as you want. I won't come back empty-handed. It's no bother at all. I'll call you as soon as I arrive. See you.*

That's it for now. No need to continue. If he'd pushed things he might have scared her away. He wanted to continue the conversation, even open a video chat, but he restrained himself.

—good night. See you, she wrote.

You are not as simple as you seem, girl, Osman said to himself, looking at the photo. Her hair hung below her shoulders, her eyebrows were drawn, her eyes were big and brown, her lips… No, they weren't *pouty,* they seemed real. Full. Here was a baby photo. The same eyes, the same eyebrows, lips…

Am I hooked already? Am I getting obsessed again? Swapping one problem for another? No, brother, nothing like that. I'll keep my distance. I'm not ready for a new relationship right now. I don't need it. I want to feel free to enjoy my…

And so Osman slowly drifted asleep.

It was evening by the time he crossed the border and arrived in Aqmescit.[7] Luman explained over the phone that they needed to finish a job for the next day. Immediately after that, they had to head out to Sudak.[8] The work there would take three days.

Suddenly Osman felt a strong urge to see Ayesha before setting out. He decided to call her.

"Ayshe, it's me, Osman, hello. How are you? I've brought your order. Can we meet in a couple of hours?"

"Oh, hello. No, that's too late. I won't leave the house at that hour. Let's meet now—if that's possible. How much do I owe you?"

"Listen, I've just arrived. I wanted to go home and change…"

"It's all right, I won't dress up either. It's not like a date… I'll just pick up my order." She studied herself in the mirror.

"Okay then. Let's meet downtown, say, in half an hour. I'll be waiting outside the café."

"Perfect. In half an hour," the girl repeated.

It took Osman twenty minutes to get there. He worried about how he looked. He was wearing traveling clothes: cargo pants, a jacket, and military-style boots. Not exactly stylish. He wished he'd been able to change into jeans or even a suit… No time. And what if she didn't like him? He remembered Sebile—she didn't like it when he was unshaven. Even a little beard made her turn away…

Should I buy flowers? But we're not dating… yet. Calm down, kid, Osman told himself. *If she likes me as I am, then she'll like me, if not, forget her…*

After a while, a girl appeared. Medium height, thin waist, eyes, eyebrows, face—everything just as in the photo. No makeup, eyelashes and lips only slightly touched up. Simply dressed: jeans, short-sleeved shirt, jacket. *This is just what you need!* he thought. He tore his gaze from her lips and looked into her eyes, which held no signs of laughter. Didn't she like him? Osman panicked.

"Hello, Ayshe?"

"Nice to meet you, Osman."

"Nice to meet you, too."

He squeezed the girl's hand and held it for a long time. "I'm delighted to meet you. Here's your order." Osman handed her the package.

"Maybe we can get a coffee at the café?" *Let's get to know each other,* he thought. *What is it? I look funny, don't I?* Suddenly he worried she might not approve of him. He was already sure he really liked her.

"Sure, but the way you're dressed, they might not let us in," the girl said smiling.

"Why not? I've been there before." Shrugging, he took Ayshe by the elbow and steered her to the café door. The waiter let her pass, but he stopped Osman, saying sternly, "We have a dress code."

"But I've been here many times…"

"It's the rule, sorry."

The girl's eyes were smiling. Seeing Osman's frustration, she suggested they try another café.

This stranger's sympathetic response heartened him.

Two hours of lively conversation were cut short by the ringing of the cell phone. It was Ayshe's mother asking her where she was.

"My family wants me back home," Ayshe said with a smile. "I have to get back home. How much do I owe you?"

"Please don't spoil things with talk of money. I'd be happy to deliver such medicine daily," Osman said.

"That won't be necessary," she answered, her voice suddenly serious.

"Why?"

"First of all, too much chocolate's not good for you. Besides, I only like Ukrainian chocolate and where would you find that here?" she asked, laughing again.

"Whatever you want, I'll find. I have to go out of town on business for a few days. Can we meet again when I get back?"

What will she say, he wondered. *What if she doesn't want to meet again? Now she's gotten what she needed. Will she turn out to be a scammer, like Luman's girlfriend? No, she doesn't look the type. There wasn't a false note in anything she said.*

She seemed to him utterly sincere.

"Okay, we'll be in touch."

"I can take you home. My car's right here."

"No need, I have a car too. But you can walk me to it."

Couldn't she have parked further away? Nothing to be done. It was time to say goodbye:

"See you soon. I'm very glad to have met you."

"Me too."

"Honestly, I'd love to just keep talking."

"Sorry. I have to go. Thanks a lot for the medicine and coffee. Goodbye."

"Goodbye. By the way, I'm a car mechanic, so if you ever have a problem with your car..."

Watching her drive off, Osman assured himself she'd surely want to meet again.

Here's the thing. She's a twenty-first-century girl who drives her own car. You won't wow her with the usual perks: a car, money. She's self-confident, serious, smart. Impressing her won't be easy.

But here was the upside: she wasn't in it for the money. She wouldn't be begging for rides to the eyebrow or nail salon. And she got his jokes... They saw eye-to-eye on so many things.

Driving home, he couldn't get her out of his head. He kept recycling their conversation, wondering if she might be the one. He hardly noticed how he got home. Everyone was watching TV, and he could sneak off to his room unnoticed. Or so he thought.

"Are you hungry, Osman?" his mother called.

"No, thanks. I had my dinner. I'm tired, I'm going to rest," he answered.

What was it like for her when she got home? I never even asked where she lives. Ah, I'll text and ask if she got home okay.

He wrote to her, and the answer came right away:

—*everything is fine, I'm at home, I'm eating my chocolate.* It was punctuated by a yellow smiley face.

Osman smiled at the emoji and replied:

Ash tatli olsun.[9] He added a row of moon shapes.

Shall I write something else? He wondered. *No, don't overdo it. Tomorrow there's work, then afterwards I'll reach out... But I already want to see her again... I've never felt quite like this. I close my eyes and she's there... Her laugh is joy itself.*

He went over every detail of the evening.

I think I'm in love.

His grandmother entered the room cautiously. Seeing that he was awake, she sat down on the edge of the bed.

"Is everything alright?" she asked the young man.

"My soul, my heart, grandmother, how do you know my feelings?"

"My eyes may not see well, but my heart feels everything, my child. You're beaming. Something's happened to you. I'd like to find out what. You drove a long way. You must be tired. Do you want anything?"

"It's alright, grandma, it's alright. Look, I'll show you something, but this should remain between us. Because I don't know how it will turn out in the end," he said, pulling up a photo of the girl on his phone. "Her name is Ayshe... We met today."

"Ah, just what you needed! Now I understand. Ayshe—that's a good name, and she looks like a nice girl. And you already like her a lot?"

Osman responded with a sigh.

"I see. She's touched your soul. May Allah give you what you want, my son. You've found what you were looking for."

1   To kiss the hand of elderly people is a Crimean Tatar old tradition

2   Haitarma—a Crimean Tatar folk dance

3   The name by which young Russian women were usually called in Crimea by Crimean Tatars who did not speak Russian well. Derived from the Russian name of Marusya, a shortened form for Maria.

4   The name of the supermarket chain

5   Citramon—a combination drug for the treatment of pain

6   "Korona," "Svitoch," and "Roshen" are Ukrainian confectionary companies

7   Aqmescit—the Crimean Tatar name for Simferopol, a city in Crimea

8   Sudak, a resort city in Crimea on the Black Sea coast, a traditional center for the production of wine

9   Ash tatli olsun—"Let the food be sweet"

Yearning

Elmira Bekirova

Adapted by Shuchi Saraswat
and Lara Stecewycz

The old man[1] had recently begun having nightmares. He would wake up crying. That very morning, he slowly lowered his feet from the bed, put on his slippers, and rose carefully. On his way to the bathroom to wash, he tried recalling his dream. After splashing water on his face, it came back to him.

The dream—or was it a memory?—was from his childhood. So distant now. It's war-time again and Crimea is occupied by the Germans. He and his friend are walking through the village. They enter a garden full of cherry trees. The cherries are ripe, and when the boys imagine the sweet and sour taste, their mouths fill with saliva. Unfortunately, picking cherries is forbidden. Suddenly, they hear German voices. The children stop and listen. The Germans have stripped off their uniforms so as not to soil them. Wearing only their undergarments, they've climbed a tree and are picking and eating cherries.

The boys look at each other. Without a word, they undress, hide their clothes in the bushes, and also climb a tree, keeping low among the leaves. Whatever cherries they find they will bring home, but if they get caught, they'll play dumb…

Assuming the boys are their own people, the Germans ignore them. Then, the policeman Gafar aqay[2] and his assistant Andrei kh----l[3] come walking down the road. They spot the Germans, exchange a few words, laugh, and move on. But something catches Gafar's eye. He stops and turns toward the tree the boys have climbed.

"Hey," he shouts. The boys skin their arms and legs shimmying down. They rush into the bushes, grab their clothes, and race away, splitting off in different directions. Bekir hears the sound of footsteps following behind him, but he continues to run. He reaches the bank of the Kacha River and throws himself in while holding his clothes above the water. Reaching the other side, he hurries towards the chaiyir.[4] That's where Gafar catches up with him.

"Where have you been?"

"Here. My mother sent me to pick beans, and that's what I'm doing." The boy tries to act nonchalant.

"You're lying. Who gave you permission to pick cherries?"

"I didn't pick any cherries. I've been here, I'm telling you…"

"He's lying, Andrei. Tie him up. Let's show him how we treat liars around here."

Andrei comes up from behind and grabs the boy, who struggles to escape. But Andrei's strong. He ties the boy to a tree.

"Tell us the truth, shitbag!"

"I have. My mother sent me to pick beans. That's what I was doing."

"You're lying, scoundrel, your friend told us you were eating cherries!"

"I don't know anything about that. I came here to get beans."

"Look at him! He lies like it's his second nature."

"Andrei, step away, let me shoot him."

The boy, seeing a gun pointed at his face, cries out: "I didn't do anything! You just wait, when our people come, they'll show you where the crayfish hibernate."

"Oh, you…"

The boy hears a gun go off. He opens his eyes and looks down. There's no blood anywhere, and nothing hurts.

"Just look at him, he didn't sell out his friend," Gafar says to Andrei. He signals to Andrei to untie the child.

The old man smiled at the dream.

After this incident, he and Gafar aqay became friends. He realized that Gafar aided the partisans, and, in the end, Bekir himself began carrying out small assignments for them. Once he even met with the partisan's commander, Vasily Cherny. He still remembers meeting on the edge of the village with a man dressed in a sailor's black peacoat. That time, Bekir provided information about the Germans in the village, answered a few questions, and delivered half a bag of provisions.

What is childhood? A wound that doesn't heal, a longing for lost innocence… The old man washed his face and put the kettle on the stove. Drinking his coffee, he thought about what he needed to do that day.

He should buy something to eat: eggs, meat, onions… He's lived alone for twenty years now. He never imagined he'd lose his wife so early. She'd always been the one to care for him. Every day for twenty years, he'd yearned for her.

Loneliness is tough, but what can you do? You live the life that Allah has given to you. The old man managed everything himself—cooked, washed his clothes, cleaned the house, swept the yard. The work was hard, sure, but he's stubborn by nature. His children—married—had invited him to live with them, but who wants to be a burden? In your own home, you go to bed when you want, you get up when you want. His children's homes are filled with the voices of his grandchildren.

"Your way of life doesn't suit me," he'd told them.

But they're good children. They visit, they look out for him. Except that he and his son still don't get along. If anything, their relationship keeps getting worse. Though they share a yard, they pass by each other without speaking. What happened? When? He can't remember. All he knows is that his son went and joined the dinjiler,[5] which the old man did not approve of.

Initially, though, the old man had been pleased. He thought: *It's better that he prefers religion to walking around and drinking with the Russian guys.* He couldn't have imagined how it would turn out. He complained to his friends: "My son began to teach me—his father—saying that I don't live correctly, that I don't do my Namaz[6] right. I observe it as my father and grandfathers did. I don't want young, foreign mullahs[7] who do not understand our way of life and who don't know what we had to overcome to teach me. Alhamdulillah,[8] we are Muslims, but we have different traditions..."

The old man frowned. He remembered the quarrel with his son and pursed his lips. *Mullahs think they can teach me... seeds that cannot see the fruit. I read a prayer, I do my Namaz, and I go to Friday prayers, but their ways of praying are quite different. When they come to the mosque, they sit apart from the others. Do they listen to vaaz[9] or not? Instead of reciting a prayer, they go to Namaz. Do they even read it at all? Is it possible to read a prayer so quickly? They perform fard[10] and then leave... and what about their beards?*

Upset by the thought of his son's goatee, the old man's hands began to tremble. Then the coffee left in the pot boiled and spilled over, making him angrier. He blamed his son for making him forget about the coffee. Now, the little pleasure he'd been looking forward to was spoiled.

When Meryem died, their son said that there was no need to perform Dua,[11] that he would go to the mosque and read the Dua himself.

"What?" the old man had asked, astonished. "Your mother dies, you bury her quickly and then you don't want even to pray for her? Go away. I don't want to see you!" he shouted.

Since then, their relationship has only deteriorated. Both were stubborn, convinced in their own righteousness.

The old man finished his coffee in a foul mood and went out into the yard. The leaves had begun to fall and needed to be swept. *Well, another autumn has arrived*, he thought. He looked up at the sky, at the white clouds chasing each other. A Russian neighbor had cut down a tree and told him, "If you need firewood, come and take it." He decided he should saw a few branches and carry them up to the stall.

The old man saw the trunk in front of his neighbor's house. There would be enough wood for him to heat the stove for a long time. He was glad that he'd found something to do. He took an ax and a cart and set to work.

It was hard but necessary work and it would make time pass more quickly. You come home so exhausted that you can hardly reach the bed—it's better than watching the clock and the door all day long...

How different things would be, how wonderful, if Meryem were still alive, he thought. No matter how much time passed, the wound from losing her had never healed. She had been his best friend, the guardian of his soul, his life partner. She was always nearby, and before he could open his mouth, while still forming the thought, she'd bring him what he needed and put it in his hand. "How did you know I needed a hammer?" the old man would ask, laughing.

"There is a board in front of you and you are doing something with nails—of course you need a hammer!" Meryem laughed back.

Remembering his wife, he felt discouraged. Everything about her had been good, except that she had spoiled their son. She never scolded him, never gave him a good spanking. He was their only son, she'd remind him. If the boy didn't like his meal, she immediately prepared another and set it in front of him. She never asked him to pick up a scoop or a hammer. The girls did all the housework: they dug the ground, made beds, planted a vegetable garden. The girls helped build the house, learning to plaster and paint as they went. Their son always had other things to do. Neither the work he did nor the money he earned was ever seen by anyone in the family. The girls married and fled to live among in-laws. His son stayed, but he was useless. He and the old man didn't understand each other then, and they still don't now.

Walking by, his son muttered, "Gathering garbage again?"

"I'm not asking for help. Do you know how much firewood costs?" the old man muttered.

It had been this way for years. When it came to hard work, his son was never around.

The old man picked up the saw and continued cutting the log. After sawing the logs, you have to haul them into the yard, cut the thicker pieces, stack them. It pays off in winter, though. You fire up the stove and enjoy the tree's gift of warmth...

The old man felt tired. He needed rest. *What's happened to me?* he thought. Until recently he didn't know what it meant to be tired. The year before last, he even climbed the Chatyrdag[12] with a group of young people. This year, though, every little movement set his heart pounding.

The old man returned to the house, made a cup of tea, found a copy of the *Kyrym*[13] newspaper folded on the table, and looked for the article about memory.

For company, he switched on the TV. ATR[14] was no longer available in Crimea without a satellite dish. Local channels offered only concerts, as if things were normal. To avoid offending anyone, they aired old movies. The exuberant music coming from the screen made the old man nervous. *The songs they sing nowadays are good-for-nothing*, he thought. He frowned and switched to another channel. He couldn't tell if what he was listening to was news. *They say they are always tormented by Ukraine, but that is a lie. They show their own devastated villages without even being ashamed, they show those who live in the same barracks that were built before the war. Well, if that was our nation, we would never wait for the government to give us houses, we would build our houses ourselves...*

The old man remembered his first house. He had no parents to help him, no money, and everything had to be purchased with ration cards.[15] When he met Meryem, he used the few kopecks[16] he had saved for marriage to buy a donkey barn from an Uzbek man. He built two more rooms, and turned it into a small house, modest even by the standards of those times. Then they moved to Tashkent. There, they bought another little house and renovated it. When they moved back to Crimea, they were able to buy a bigger house with gas, water, and other modern conveniences.

Ours is a nation that does not ask anyone for anything and knows how to survive. We moved to Crimea, lived in basements; we suffered and got help from no one, but look—we managed to build houses, and compared to those we lived in before we were deported, they are better and more comfortable. Some of us even put up three- and four-story houses. I'm proud of my nation, maşallah![17] Whenever I hear that one of us has opened his own business, I'm genuinely delighted. We all work. We all have an opinion on this or that issue. Such a nation cannot easily be destroyed...

The old man looked through the newspaper. Sounds of explosions came from the TV. Zvezda[18] was showing a film about the war. "Oh, you," the old man cursed, "for seventy years they've been killing the Germans. They show us one soldier killing a whole crowd of Germans. If that were really so, how was it possible that this government lost three or four times as many people as the Germans? What drivel."

The old man's thoughts drifted back to the war. He remembered people were taken to dig trenches near Akyar.[19] He went to his mother's place, but the minute he had the chance, he ran away. The Qazaqs[20] chased him. During the German occupation, the Qazaqs served as their guards. After he escaped, he ran again to the Kacha River, which was covered in scattered reeds. He stepped on a cut reed, and it entered through the bottom of his foot and out through the top. He pulled it out with some difficulty, wrapped the wound with his shirt, and limped home. But the wound began to fester and his leg swelled massively, and soon he could not walk on it at all.

A German living in their house—they called him Futumaister—assessed the situation, and took him to the hospital immediately. There they washed the wound, applied some ointment, and released him, telling him to come again. This was the "harm" caused by the Germans. Soon, his foot healed. Later, another German soldier saved him, this time from shelling. He'd been in an open field when the bombing began. Seeing him, a German soldier ran out of the trench and dragged him to a safe place. *Such Germans as they show now in the movies I have never seen. Yes, they killed the Communists and those who resisted them. But this was war...*

On TV, it was always the German soldiers who were killed. The old man got angry and turned it off. He picked up the newspaper again, put on his glasses, moved from the table to the sofa, and leaned back. *I'll read and rest*, he thought. After reading for a while, he closed his eyes and fell asleep.

Either because of the article or because he had been thinking a lot about the past, he again dreamt of his former life.

He's a small child and his father, who can't accept life on a collective farm, leaves them to move to Bakhchysarai. He wants to run after his father, but his mother holds his hand tightly. "Don't worry, my son, your father will return and bring you a toy." She fooled him. He's yearned for his father ever since.

The sound of his own sobs woke him. His dream made him realize he missed his father and mother very much. He looked around and saw that he was back in the present. He took a deep breath. He wasn't as tired as he'd been, but his heart ached. He stroked his chest as if trying to smooth out the pain with his hand. He returned to cutting the wood. He'd gather a bundle to keep in the house.

Had there been grandchildren around, they might have helped him carry the firewood. But they were gone. His daughter-in-law had quarreled with her husband and left him. It was his son's fault. Leaving the house, she explained, "I will not quit my job. I have children to raise. If I wear a hijab, I will lose my job. I won't make my daughter wear the hijab. She will study. I studied, got an education, and dressed in Soviet-era clothes, all while following our customs. In my opinion, faith in Allah should be in the heart, not in clothes. If you read Namaz five times instead of working, we will starve, I am sorry to say." The old man missed the children. They came, of course, for holidays, but not to visit him.

"Hello, neighbor! How are you, your health?"

The old man turned to see where the voice had come from. His neighbor Anatoly stood next to him.

"Ah, hello, Tolik,[21] I'm fine, as you can see. I'm working slowly."

The old man noticed that his neighbor's eyes were wet from tears. They'd had a good relationship since his arrival in Crimea. The two men helped each other in times of need. The old man worked at construction sites all his life and could do a lot on his own. Neighbors came and went. As the Crimean Tatars returned to Crimea, they found among them actual and invented relatives.

If earlier they were afraid of showing their emotions, now they look at us with hatred, as if they have gone off the rails, thought the old man. *But those who arrived later—those who came from Luhansk-Donetsk—are completely devoid of humanity. We want a peaceful life, to build our own state, to live comfortably, to build houses, to plant gardens. They, on the other hand, create trouble, file false claims. Those who do not agree with the authorities are imprisoned, regardless of their age.*

The old man looked angrily at the door of the opposite house. *Baba Shura was a good woman and when she died, her children rented the house out to people from the eastern regions![22] Every day there is a scandal, booze, yelling and fighting. Where do they get money to pay for rent if they don't work and drink all day long every day... Or does the government pay them money for being, as they say, "migrants"?!*

The old man took a deep breath. His hands were working and his thoughts were swarming in his head like bees. Everything was spinning.

As for money, when the new government came,[23] they said they would reha-bilitate our people and so they did… But still, I can't take a piece of that useless paper. They will give us only 500 rubles.[24] My documents, they claim, were not preserved in the archives. But in my passport, my birthplace is quite clearly written—the Bakhchysarai district, the village of Kalymtay.[25] What other evidence do they need? If they want to know whether I was deported or not, they can find out from the police. Weren't they the ones to give us passports? The city of Tashkent in Uzbekistan, and before that the Samarkand region. When it comes to themselves, they will find a way out of any situation. If necessary, they'll even pass new laws. When it comes to us, they'll look for some kind of additional information and put obstacles in our way for everything.

They banned our May 18th commemorations.[26] People would gather, meet with each other, share memories, perform Dua[27] for those who died while in exile or in transit to distant places. And the authorities would not let us gather. The only gatherings they allowed were meetings of fellow villagers. So we had to gather in secret. Who knows—maybe tomorrow or the day after tomorrow, they will ban those meetings as well.

The old man finished sawing and laid the cut firewood in his cart. He unloaded it by his front door. Eventually, he would transfer the logs inside to the barn. He raised his head and looked at the sun. *It must be noon already.* He decided to have a bite, even though he had no appetite. If he didn't eat, his stomach would ache.

He'd suffered from stomach problems since childhood. The cause was clear: starvation when he was just a kid. Later, the doctor explained it to him: "There are tissues inside the stomach that help us digest food, but your stomach is smooth inside like a knee. If you eat heavy, bitter, sour, or fried food, you will suddenly feel pain, and an ulcer may burst."

Meryem was very serious when it came to his stomach problems. Every day she prepared fresh, light meals. His ulcers healed well, and no surgery was needed. But suffering from starvation in his youth left its mark. What terrible days those had been! His stomach would twist with hunger, but there was nothing to eat anywhere. He did have his mother who could say: "Here, my dear, eat this."

The old man teared up. It looked like his sister had taken his gro-cery card without his knowing it. She was eating both his food and her own. Sometimes, after giving him some of her food, she would say, "Go work, go get a job, earn money. I have to take care of my child. As you can see, he is still small and I can't work, there is no one to leave him with." This drove him out of the barracks.

Their mother had always been in poor health. She died in the train wagon as they were being deported. That day she wanted some water. When the train stopped, the old man, then in his teens, took a gügüm[28] and went looking for water. While he was out, the train started to move. He ran after the wagon, threw the gügüm at the open door, but wasn't able to climb back on himself. A few wagons passed. Finally, seeing a pair of hands extended out to him, and with the last of his strength, he reached out, and the hands hoisted him into the wagon.

The train ran without stopping for a long time. He continued his journey among people from the neighboring village. They even shared a little of their food with him. When the train finally stopped, he hurried back to his own wagon, but his mother was already gone, carried away. She had died in the meantime—from hunger, from grief, from fear... who knows? He didn't get to say goodbye to her, didn't see her for the last time, never got to ask her to forgive him for all the times he'd been wrong. Since then, he never ceased yearning for his mother. The old man began weeping again. *Now I've lived two years longer than my mother, and still the burning pain does not leave me. If I'd been with her, I could've said goodbye and wouldn't feel so much hurt to this day.*

The old man recalled the days before the deportations began. His mother, who worked on a collective farm, had been unable to achieve her quota. The other women barely worked and would return home laughing and singing. His mother, however, had been unable to finish even half her quota. With much care, she was loosening the ground, making it light and airy. He often joined her in the field to help out. Once, the women laughed at him, saying to his mother: "Emine, look, your assistant is coming." And he, being only a child, picked up a stick and chased after them, which only made them laugh even harder.

He cried and his mother stroked his head and caressed him. He missed his mother very much. His heart ached. He felt sick.

He leaned against the back of the sofa. It was cool and quiet inside the house. He found a tablet of Valocardine[29] and swallowed it. *It will pass now*, he said to himself. *If I tell the children, they will immediately call for an ambulance. So much fuss. Do I need an ambulance? No, it should pass.* He closed his eyes and fell asleep.

In his dream, he saw his mother. She was sitting outside the house wearing a kerchief over her head, cleaning the beans in her apron, singing softly, "Ismail, my dear, where are you, where is your grave?" She often sang this song, composed during the years of famine. She raised her head, saw her son and smiled: "Where are you going? I am waiting for you. Your father called you. Terlemez Abdulla[30] will go to Bakhchysarai on his cart and you'll go with him. You will take beans, cucumbers, and then come back..."

The old man woke with a start to a loud knock at the door. *Although I do not want to leave this sweet dream*, he thought, *it would be rude not to answer. My son wouldn't get up to open the door, even if the world were on fire.*

"I'm coming, I'm coming," he shouted, wondering who it could be. When he opened the door, he saw his new neighbor, who had moved in recently.

"Grandfather, lend me thirty rubles to buy bread. I'll give it back. When I get money, I'll give it back."[31]

Had his neighbor been a good person, he'd gladly have given him money. But the man was an alcoholic who drank everything away. The old man had believed him initially, and had lent freely, but then saw that his neighbor didn't work and was always drunk. Since then, he began refusing, saying that he had no money himself. Still, his neighbor continued to come.

"I'm a pensioner. From where can I get any money?" asked the old man. "You're young, you go to work. Why are you drinking? Your wife is young, pregnant. Go to work, live like a man. If you're in need, I'll help. But I won't give you money for vodka."[32]

"Oh, you, Tatar face, you bitch, damn you, you think you can teach me?! Traitors. Fuck you. Because of you, we have the war. Because of you, I lost my house!"[33] The drunk raised his hand as if he wanted to hit the old man.

Hearing these blasphemous words, the old man became furious. All the anger and dissatisfaction he'd felt throughout his life overwhelmed him.

"Are you a fool? I didn't invite the war into your house, you wanted it yourself. You are all like that, you've freeloaded your entire life. They gave you a house for free, and it wasn't enough: you wanted more. Here, you also live for free."[34]

The old man's heart began to beat faster. Just as on May 18th, when their whole sweet life was taken away, this worthless bastard had torn him from a sweet dream. And for what? For money to buy more vodka. The old man grabbed a log from the cart and hit the Qazaq on the head, then he seized him by the throat and began to choke him and beat him. All the yearning, resentment, anguish, bitterness, and rage that had accumulated throughout his life moved through his hands. He wanted revenge.

"What have you lost? You have any idea how much I've lost, because of you? Who will give me back my childhood, my mother, my father? My father was taken away to work and I never saw him again. My mother died on the train while being deported. As a child, I was always hungry. My friend Ibraim swelled from hunger and eventually died, as did his mother when breastfeeding her child. Have you ever seen such things? A whole family dying... seven men. We don't want war, we need land for houses, vegetable gardens, land to plant and grow food. It is you for whom nothing is ever enough, you want more money for vodka, your nation has taken over here, the whole of your world has arisen here, and *I* am the guilty one? *I* am the traitor? Zhorka now lives in my house. When we were young, we, together, caught crayfish in the Kacha River, and now he acts like he does not know me. Because he lives in my house. And you're the same. Worse. You've come to my land, you live here, drink here, and now you call me a traitor?"[35]

The old man, lost in rage, slowly came to himself. He looked into the horrified eyes of the Qazaq, spat into his bloody face, and let him go. He took a deep breath to calm his pounding heart, and walked into the yard where he stretched out on the bench.

...He is a young boy. His father bends down and lifts him high with his strong arms, the way he used to when placing him on the back of a cow and taking him to the village. Suddenly, the old man felt very light, as if his father were carrying him upstairs.

Safe behind the fence, the Qazaq wiped away his blood, while his wife asked what happened. "I was beaten by an old man. We should've moved to Krasnodar[36] or Rostov."[37] His wife stared at her husband, open-mouthed.

Alone again, the old man realized that he was leaving this world.

"I'm dying." Having spoken those words, he exhaled his last breath.

A little boy sits on a cow, and they're headed toward the village. His father walks beside them, holding the boy to keep him from falling. The days are happy. Soon, the village is visible. His mother is standing near the house. She shields her eyes against the sun with her hand as she waits for her son to return.

At last, I am with those I've yearned for, was his final thought, flashing like a spark from a dying fire that dims, then goes out.

1   The old man's name is Bekir
2   Aqay—uncle
3   *Kh----l* is a derogatory term for "a Ukrainian"
4   Chaiyir—a garden in the forest where Crimean Tatars used to graft trees
5   Dinjiler—believers adhering to strict dogmatic rules; a type of Islam unusual to the Crimean Tatars
6   Namaz—a prayer in Islam
7   Mullah—Islamic cleric and expert on the Qur'an and religious rites among Muslims
8   Alhamdulillah—an expression from a chapter in Fatıha ın Holy Qur'an
9   Vaaz—a sermon
10 Fard—an obligatory part of prayer
11 To perform Dua—pray
12 Chatyrdag—a mountain range located in the southern part of the Crimean Peninsula 10 km above sea level (the fifth highest mountain in Crimea)
13 *Kyrym*—a national newspaper of the Crimean Tatars in the Crimean Tatar language
14 ATR was a national TV station in Crimea for Crimean Tatar culture, language, and news. Following Russia's occupation of Crimea in 2014, the channel was forced to stop broadcasting.
15 In the Soviet Union during and after WWII, a ration card would allow its owner to receive 125g of bread.
16 A kopeck—a coin in the Soviet currency system

17 Maşallah—Well done!

18 Zvezda ("star")—the name of the Russian TV channel

19 Akyar—the Crimean Tatar name for Sevastopol, a city in the southwest of the Crimean Peninsula

20 Qazaqs—Cossacks, the name used by the Crimean Tatars to refer to the Russians

21 Tolik—a short form for Anatoly

22 "People from the eastern regions"—a reference to the migrants from the east of Ukraine, primarily Donetsk and Luhansk, who moved to Crimea in the wake of Russia's occupation of the peninsula. The settlers usually supported Russia and its military aggression against Ukraine.

23 A reference to the government that rehabilitated the Crimean Tatars after decades of repression and exile following their deportation in 1944

24 Ruble—Soviet currency

25 Kalymtay—a village in the Bakhchysarai District of Crimea (modern Tenyste)

26 May 18, 1944—the date of deportation of Crimean Tatars from Crimea, a day of national mourning

27 To perform Dua—pray

28 Gügüm—a jug; a water vessel traditionally used in Crimea

29 Valocardine—a medical product to relieve anxiety, stress, mild heart pain

30 Terlemez Abdulla—a nickname that means "the non-sweating Abdullah." In villages, almost every person had a nickname, and sometimes a person was known more by his/her nickname than by his/her last name.

31 Originally written in Russian: "Дед, займи тридцатку, хлеб купить, я отдам, вот деньги получу, отдам."

32 This part of the text was intentionally written in poor Russian to show that the old Crimean Tatar man did not know this language well; his native language was Crimean Tatar, and Russian was imposed by the Soviet regime. "Я пенсионер. Откуда у меня деньги? Ты молодой, иди, работай. Зачем пьёшь? Жена молодой, беременный, работай, живи как человек. Надо, памагу. На водка деньга не дам."

33 Originally written in Russian: "Ах ты морда татарская, с...ка, б...ть. Учить меня будешь?! Предатели. Я вас ... Да из-за вас у нас война, из-за вас я дом потерял."

34 This part of the text was intentionally written in poor Russian: "Ты дурак? Я твой дом войну не звал. Ты сам хател. Вы все такие, всю жизнь на халяву живёте. Там тебе дом на халяву дали, мала паказалась, ещё захотел...Здесь на халяву живёшь..."

35 This part of the text was intentionally written in poor Russian: "Ты
потерял тавариш? А что я потерял знаиш, нет? Мой детство, мой мама,
папа кто вернёт? Папа трудармия забрали, болше иво не видел, мама
в дорога умер, я голодный ходил, мой друг Кирпишка Ибраим апух ат
голада, умер, иво мама умер, малинкий рибонок мёртвый мама грудь
сасал. Ты такой видел? Целый семья умирал… Сем челавек. Нам вайна
не нада, нам земля нада, дом строить, агарод, сад сажат… то вам всё
мала, на водка больше денег захател, вес свой нация, вес свой мир суда
пазвал, и я типер винаватый? Я придател? Мой дом типер Жорка живёт.
Малинкий был, вместе на Кача рак ловили, а типер он меня низнает.
Патаму что в мой дом живёт… И ты такой жа. Дажа хужа. Пришёл моя
земля, живёшь, пьёшь и я тебе ишо предатель?…"

36 Krasnodar—a city in Russia

37 Rostov—a city in Russia

The Walnut Tree
and the Geranium

Zera Bekirova

Adapted by William Pierce

"Beyan, hello! Can you hear me? I got my visa. I'm traveling back home now, but you'll see me very soon. I'll let you know when I arrive as soon as I've bought the ticket. Tell me, what would you like me to bring for you from Crimea?" Unable to contain her joy, Ayshe had bounded out of the consulate in Odesa and called her friend, who had long ago asked her to visit and even sent an official invitation. She and Beyan had known each other for more than twenty years but still hadn't met in person. They had exchanged letters and recently talked by phone, but that was it. A few years ago, Ayshe was surprised to find a letter in her mailbox from "Bella Alexandrova." Who was Bella Alexandrova? It was Beyan, who, between the lines, tried to explain why she was using a new name now. In Bulgaria, not only were people's names changing, but the villages' names as well. A matter of the political climate. Just like in Crimea…

"I'm very happy, Ayshe! Congratulations! Please bring a bag of topsoil and two walnut trees, if it's not too much trouble!"

Beyan's request confused Ayshe. Oh, Allah. Is there no topsoil there? Are there no walnut trees growing? According to her geography knowledge, the climate in Bulgaria should be fairly similar to the one in Crimea. They were both on the Black Sea coast!

"Beyan, my dear, is that what you really want? Maybe you want something else?"

"It will be enough if you could bring some soil and walnut trees! I wouldn't ask for anything else."

On her way back from Odesa to Simferopol, Ayshe stopped at her mother's house located in a village to tell her that she was going on a long journey. After asking Beyan what she would like from Crimea, she now asked her mother, "What would you like me to bring for you from Bulgaria?" As always, her mother read the prayer for her daughter's good journey, then said, "Bring me a pound of Bulgarian cheese if you can."

Ayshe was surprised again. "Mom, Bulgarian cheese isn't in short supply. You can buy it in any store."

"Oh, but the taste is different. In Bulgaria, they make real cheese from sheep's milk. I've eaten that cheese many times and I still remember its taste. If you don't bring any, I won't be offended. It will be more than enough that you come back alive and well, my daughter!"

Ayshe told her mother that Beyan had asked her to bring two walnut trees and a bag of topsoil. "I'll get them from our garden. As far as I understand, Beyan's ancestors were from a village very much like ours." Ayshe took a shovel and went into the yard. She filled one bag with soil, then continued on to the garden. Every year in autumn, the crows carried walnuts and hid them in the freshly turned soil. Ayshe had watched them so many times, it was like a movie. Putting aside a walnut, a crow would dig a hole, then look around before burying the nut, to be sure no one could see. There was something in it Ayshe didn't understand. Was the crow saving nuts for winter or planting them so trees would grow? Either way, the bird was very smart. The crows must have chosen only the best walnuts because each spring nearly every garden had five or six walnuts shooting up. Ayshe and her siblings used to replant them in the wasteland behind their house and tend to the whole grove. And in time, they were gathering bags of nuts. The neighbors always got a "neighbor's share." Their late grandmother had taught them this. She'd say, "Neighbors have a right to everything that grows in the garden."

Ayshe shared the walnuts not only with people in the neighborhood but also with friends living in Turkey. They were so happy to get them. "The taste of Crimean nuts is quite different," they used to say. But Beyan wasn't asking her to bring nuts, she wanted seedlings. Ayshe picked two tender ones, digging carefully so as not to damage the roots. Anything larger wouldn't be allowed at customs, it would be removed. Customs officers were always looking for a reason to say no. They'd claim, "It's forbidden, it's forbidden." They rummaged through people's luggage and removed a lot of items.

Ayshe wrapped the seedlings in the hem of one of her dresses, cloaked the bag of topsoil in the same dress, and then tucked it at the bottom of her suitcase. She laid two more dresses on top. And soon the day arrived. As she was leaving, she tried to imagine the melancholy of those who'd decided a hundred or a hundred and fifty years ago to leave forever. How were they able to give up their nests? What did they take with them? A feeling of deprivation suffused her. Through the small windows of the plane, the Black Sea was visible. The journey took several hours. No one knew how long an emigrant's journey lasted—it might be weeks or months, in a convoy of ox carts by land; in boats crossing the sea...

Her thoughts were interrupted by the voice of a flight attendant, "We're starting our initial descent. In thirty minutes, we'll arrive in Varna, Bulgaria."

"How was the trip?" Beyan asked. "My friend, why such a short visit? You prepared for so long—traveled such a long way, spent a great deal of money. Who comes out for just three days?" She added a strange sibilance to her words. They sounded very funny.

"That's just how it turned out," Ayshe said. "I was barely able to take the days off. But this won't be my last time, inshallah.[1] I'll be back. Now tell me the plan. You said you wanted to see a few places."

"Tomorrow we'll go to the Tepresh Festival[2] in Dobrich. You'll meet a lot of people there. We'll visit Hadzhioglu Pazarshyk the morning after, and in the evening I'll take you to our village. We'll plant the walnut seedlings you brought, and sprinkle fresh Crimean soil over the graves."

The main square in Dobrich, even early in the morning, was crowded. Old women sat in a row, beautifully dressed, their aprons tied in front and their maramas[3] draped over their heads. They were waiting for the spectacle to come. Crimean dishes were laid out to attract buyers—peshlokum, kobete, sariburma, dzhantiks. And Beyan, taking Ayshe's hand, went around introducing her to everyone, but with the music, the chanting, and the loud rustle of people moving through the square, Ayshe had trouble catching their words. She got so tired that, without waiting for dinner, she lay down on the bed prepared for her and fell straight to sleep.

In the morning, she felt much better. Beyan had already made coffee, and the table was set with bread and cheese. As soon as Ayshe saw the cheese, she remembered her mother's request. "I can't forget to buy cheese," she reminded herself. "My mom will be waiting for it." But she must have said it aloud. Beyan answered right away, "Of course. We'll get it at the market. Let's buy the kind that comes in an iron box. That will be easier for you to carry home. Our plan has changed a little. Last night my friend called. She is a poet from Varna. She wants to meet you. So, let's walk around the city together, and she and I will take you to the famous Golden Sands beach."

"Don't be offended, Beyan, but I really want to go to the village and see the life there. Let's meet your friend another time."

Beyan's mood was spoiled, but she didn't want to let on. "Let's do it this way. My younger brother will go to the cemetery with us. We'll put soil on the graves and plant the walnuts on both sides of the cemetery gate. Then he'll take you to the village while I briefly visit my friend. I'll feel ashamed if I don't go. I promised. But I'll join you after lunch."

All three of them did their ablutions and set out for the cemetery. But a few feet from the gate, they heard their neighbor's voice, "How are you, is everything okay? That's wonderful, Beyan! Your qisim[4] arrived from Crimea. Come visit us!"

Hearing the woman's dialect—especially the word "qisim"—Ayshe shuddered. She'd heard that expression when she was little, but one would rarely say it in Crimea anymore.

"This too is a village," Beyan said. "Everyone knows everybody's business." She laughed, looking at Ayshe. "The women on this block already know what's about to be cooked in the cauldron on the block over. When she called you my qisim, I remembered that the oldest person in our village died, the wife of a man named Murat. She was qisim to us also. Let's stop in and see him for just a few minutes to express our condolences. The old man will be happy. They used to follow the Crimean tradition of going straight home after a funeral and not being seen by anyone."[5]

Murat's house was at the edge of the village. His wife's passing had left him there alone. As soon as emigration became allowed, their two sons had gone to Europe.

"Hello, Murat aqay!"[6] Beyan kissed her elder's hand. "Pray for peace. You've buried Aunt Mapuse."

"Peace be upon you, daughter!" the old man said. "Who's beside you? I don't recognize her."

Ayshe kissed the man's hand[7] also and touched her forehead. She recalled that in her childhood people had expressed condolences in this same way, by saying, "Pray for peace," and answered not with a reference to *friends* like now, but more formally, "Peace be upon you."

"This is my friend, Ayshe," Beyan said. "She's traveled here from Crimea."

"Can she speak the language? They say Crimean Tatar is already forgotten in Crimea."

"I know my mother tongue, of course," Ayshe said, offended.

Murat's show of surprise made everyone laugh.

"She brought some soil with her, and two walnut trees," Beyan said. "We'll take them to the cemetery."

The old man's eyes filled with tears. He clearly wanted to say something, but his voice was trembling, so he raised his hands and prayed.

They took the main street through the village. On both sides, the houses were low, with tiled roofs and small windows painted blue. It warmed her heart when she saw a village mosque, but the minaret here was uncanny. Was she in Crimea... or not in Crimea? For centuries, people who'd been separated from their homeland built their own Crimeas. They built new villages from scratch, first erecting a mosque and choosing a mullah. This leader was entrusted with his congregation's spiritual life and also the children's education. Each family built a copy of the house they'd left behind in Crimea.

After opening the gates and entering the cemetery, Ayshe, Beyan, and her younger brother read the Ikhlas[8] from the Qur'an three times.

"Is this an old cemetery?" Ayshe asked, surprised at how new the tombstones looked.

"No," Beyan said, "there was a campaign to convince every citizen that we're part of a single nation and share a single religion—and overnight the original cemetery was destroyed. Nobody knows anything about it. The graves belonged to Crimean Tatars—my grandmother, my great-grandfather, their parents were all buried there. Some tombstones had the tamga[9] symbol. But they were removed. Even the traces were erased. So this is a new one. We've found and collected the bones left in the old cemetery and reburied them here."

Beyan walked to the grave of her mother, who passed away two years ago. She put some Crimean soil over it and spread the rest among the other graves. "Now let's plant the nuts at the entrance. My grandfather said that when they were leaving Crimea, they dug up fresh, green walnut seedlings and carried them along. All the way they watered the roots of the young trees so they wouldn't dry out. My grandfather was five or six at the time, and after the seedings were planted here, where they settled, he watered them every day. Of course, they grew. But they didn't produce a harvest. My grandfather was always sad about that. He said, 'They're like us. They yearn.' Those words seemed like part of an implausible fairy tale as if the trees were somehow conscious and knew what it was to pine for another place. Many seasons later, a few nuts appeared—and that was the year my grandfather died. Ever since I've dreamed of bringing walnut trees from Crimea and planting them in memory of my grandfather and all our homesick ancestors."

Ayshe left the cemetery broken-hearted. O, fate! The thread of destiny! To have been born in an earthly paradise and then be displaced thousands of miles from it. To find no peace, even in the grave...

"Dear Ayshe, walk on to the village with Gevat," Beyan said. "I'll join you this evening—and in the meantime, I'll get the cheese for your mother. Sheep's milk cheese, yes? We'll return from the village very late tonight, and you leave so early tomorrow. We won't have time."

Gevat took over as a guide. "I'll take you to the village called Tatar Water. An old man there speaks very good Crimean Tatar."

"What a name," Ayshe said, and asked how the village came to be called Tatar Water. Gevat laughed and shrugged.

When they arrived, a familiar feeling came over her. It was once again as if old pictures, postcards, and engravings of Crimean landscapes were coming to life before her eyes: the tiling on the houses, the architectural style, the mosque, and people's open, sincere faces. Gevat stopped at a low house.

"Aunt Remzie, are you home?"

"Welcome, my son. Yes, I'm fine here. I don't go anywhere now." She came out, a pale-faced woman with a white scarf tied around her head and a white apron around her middle. "Oh, another guest. Come in, come in. I'll quickly put the cezve on the fire and make some coffee."

Ayshe hugged her, kissed the old woman on her cheeks and hand. She reminded Ayshe of her own grandmother. And her parlor was furnished exactly as in the old paintings—embroidered towels hung on the walls, her typical Crimean sofa covered with white embroidered blankets, straw pillows on top of those, and a square qona,[10] the kind of dinner table that came from only one place. Right under it, potted flowers lined the windows—all geraniums.

Grandma Remzie, when she heard that Ayshe came from Crimea, began talking about her family's past.

"Our old people were very rich. They had gold, flocks of sheep, horses. But during the occupation, their property was looted. As soon as the infidels appeared in our village, my grandfather and great-grandfather decided to leave and gave the household the task of pulling everything together very quickly. My grandfather stuffed gold in bags. They could only take their clothes and documents with them, that's all. But my grandmother loved flowers—most of all she loved geraniums." Remzie used the word gulidan[11] which had fallen out of use in Crimea. "Without telling my grandfather, she took a gulidan out of a pot and hid it in her clothes. The customs officers searched everything as people boarded the ship. They found my grandfather's gold and currency and confiscated all of it. They even took away passports. So, my family arrived in this village with nothing. Their shoes quickly wore out, they lost weight. There wasn't even a village here in those days—refugees weren't allowed in the villages! They were taken to empty places. Wilderness. But my grandfather gathered together a few men, and they began to dig a well. The people from the surrounding villages laughed, but that didn't stop them. Our men dug for weeks, and at last they hit fresh water. Once you have that, you can build houses, plant gardens, take care of animals. The people who'd ridiculed them started coming by to ask for a taste of 'Tatar water.'"

"My grandmother's geraniums withered almost to nothing, but she revived them with water from the new well. She made a clay pot and was finally able to plant the gulidan. It was a miracle of Allah. If you will, even a blind eye can shed a tear; the flower came back to life. My great-grandmother bequeathed it to anyone returning to Crimea—they should take her geranium back with them. But no one's been destined to do that, and now it wouldn't work. The flower has become part of our heritage." Grandma Remzie pointed to the geraniums on her windowsills. "We all grow new ones from cuttings, generation by generation."

After the coffee and conversation, Gevat and Ayshe walked around the village, visiting many homes. It was late evening when Beyan joined them. By the time they returned home, it was midnight.

On the way back, Gevat's phone rang.

"All right, all right," Gevat said. "We'll come to you, don't worry." He turned to Ayshe. "Aunt Remzie wants us to return for a few minutes. She has something to give you."

Grandma Remzie was waiting for them outside. When Gevat's car stopped, she begged Ayshe, "My dear daughter, I am the only one left of our family. My husband passed away and my son died in an accident last year. I have nobody. I want to fulfill the wish of my old grandmother. I've lived with it for so long but had lost hope. Take this gulidan to Crimea! I planted it just recently, and it already has one bud."

Ayshe took the pot and promised to plant the gulidan in Crimea.

She couldn't sleep until morning. So many feelings and impressions stirred in her. And she was anxious about the upcoming trip.

"What's in your suitcase? Open it!" The woman's voice was very rough.

"Just personal belongings."

"Plants can't be taken across the border. Especially in a flower pot filled with the soil. And what's this? Cheese? Dairy products are also prohibited."

"I brought the cheese for my mother. There's not much. And the plant is from an old woman in Bulgaria, part of her inheritance in a way.

I promised I would take it back to Crimea. I'm begging you. If there's a fine, I'll pay. Just please don't take the plant from me."

"You need to choose," the customs officer said sharply. "Either the plant—removed from the pot, with no soil—or the block of cheese. I won't let both through."

"Okay, take away the cheese. My mother will understand. And the flower needs to be delivered."

The officer liked this. She even seemed to smile.

The moment she got home, Ayshe planted the flower in an empty pot and watered it well. Then in the morning, at the city's main market, she looked for a cheese marked "Bulgarian" and put it in the bag she'd brought back with her, covered in Cyrillic inscriptions. Retrieving the potted geranium, she went to visit her mother.

"You see, I told you, the taste of cheese from Bulgaria is completely different. It tastes even better with coffee. Thank you, my daughter."

Allah's forgiveness for the lie, but Ayshe didn't have the heart to tell her mother the truth.

"Where did you get this plant? I have similar ones here, you know. What color are the flowers?"

Mother and daughter talked the whole day through.

When she was ready to go back to the city, Ayshe noticed a new fragrance in the house. It was Grandma Remzie's gulidan—and the flowers were snow white!

1   Inshallah—"I hope"
2   Tepresh—Crimean Tatar spring festivities
3   Maramas—national embroidered scarves for elderly women
4   Qisim—relative
5   According to a national tradition, the Crimean Tatars go straight home after funerals to avoid bringing misfortune to others.
6   Murat aqay—Uncle Murat
7   To kiss the hand of elderly people is a Crimean Tatar tradition
8   Ikhlas—the last prayer of the Qur'an
9   Tamga—a national and cultural symbol, representing the Crimean Tatars' historical statehood, identity, and resistance to oppression
10 Qona—a national low dinner table
11 Gulidan—geranium

Zulbiye Sattarova

Adapted by Ha Jin

Dawn

A golden circle comes out of the horizon,
lighting up the surface of the earth.
The world has changed, struck by a miracle.
Plants are bathed in dew.
A nightingale throbs in the garden
as if admitting that trees and rivers are its friends,
that all living things stir with zikr.[1]
Smells and sounds are wafting in the air,
the colors of young greens vibrant with brilliance.
Our hearts are full of sweet feelings.
Beauty is the reward Allah gives us,
so we should all be grateful.

---

1 Zikr—ritual remembrance of Allah, joy of dervishes

Perdalez. Meeting

Spring is a pretty good season
when people fall in love with warm climate.
Everywhere there're pleasant smells, soft voices,
blossoming trees and loamy earth.
Oh, what a deceptive world
which is so well-made!

Winter also has its beauty
everything becomes clean and white,
snowflakes, soft and clean,
like wintery flowers flying around.
Oh, what a deceptive world,
which is so well-made!

Oh, this deceptive world.
When winter and spring meet
nature changes thoroughly.
All snow is gone, green not here yet.
Everything looks ugly.
Oh, this deceptive world,
where worse can become worst.

Crimea

Crimea is a peninsula
celebrated in destans.[2]
Is there a similar country
in the world?
Its mountains and prairies
are gorgeous.
Its springs and autumns
surpass any praise.
Fragrant air floats like
balm for the soul.
The blue-blue sea laps
sandy shores. Again,
the bountiful harvest
fills gardens and fields.
It's green everywhere.
What an emerald country!

2 Destan—a legend; a lyric and epic work

Cranes

Sounds come from heaven
as the cranes fly away.
They are moving in rows
struggling for a long flight.
Those birds have left their homeland
and now are heading home.
They were forced to be away,
to go to a distant land.
They have a hard journey ahead.
There's no other way for them,
all they have is patience.
Hard times will pass.
They have bonded together
and will be back again.

* * * * * *

I feel trapped in an endless desert,
where there's no footprint, no wind
and there's only hot sand,
where wild bests hide in bushes.
When it's right time, they rush out to attack.
Snakes also crawl around
in secret for prey.
Moans shatter deadly silence,
petrifying the heart.
It will rain heavily
and earth will turn green again.
So good ideas and thoughts will burgeon again,
again filling yearning hearts with faith.

Maye Safet
Adapted by Diane Mehta

Khan's Palace

The bandit-state unfeathered the seminary
and made it a madhouse,
sacked the Khan's palace—
it fit so beautifully against the contour
of mountains in Bakhchysarai.
The bandit-state, unsatiated,
chewed so many corpses.
Our ancestors lament in their graves.

What perfidy to hack tiles off
monuments we loved, to erase
our homeland, our ancient ornaments,
our science of verse, labor of equations
explaining the universe that holds us all.
Grammar was on our tongues, once.
They killed the study of logic and good laws
but slow is murder for we remember it still.
How bitter are these absences,
filthy our memory of blood-burning
deportations. We lost the land and speech itself
was lost, abandoned to the land.
They cut its tongue out, and language,
starved for conversation, began
to lose its mind. We sing folk songs
so Crimea lives even as we disappear.

Oh, those hewn trees under the snow!
They script our land with invisible calligraphy;
their medieval branches are rich with our history.
(Even gold is worthless compared to this.)
Some say: do not touch the tender building.
It will return to soil on its own terms.
The architecture of the palace is a cosmos.
It casts a spell on the land-bandits
who turned it all into a madhouse.

Swarming

Fruit of spring,
harvest of every living thing
sweetens the air.

Peaches sprung on branches,
almond trees with pollinating bees,
Fruit blushes like young brides.
The scent blinds your eyes!

Forests stir so early.
Creeks chatter like children's laughter.
People build piers by the lakesides.
All the lakes overflow with snowmelt
racing to the sea yelling the news—
spring has come to Crimea!

Forget your worries—
go out and catch the wind,
get dizzy, train your eyes to love
everything, savor the mild air
swirling there, so beautiful
is our homeland,
so holy is Crimea our motherland.

Dust!

Oh, mother, why do you wake me up so early?
Even wind shivers, and ice wishes it were colder
to keep itself from breaking—

A savage man yells as if he were hunting,
we the prey, but what have we done wrong?
He grabs my bag from my hands, kicks it away.
You replace it with some flour in a box
(for later, you say).

Black-eyed Qarakoz,[1]
his weeping beast of a dog,
resembles three-headed Cerberus—
it howls at us, flashing its shiny teeth,
waiting to tear into me.
I don't know if right now is late
last night or early morning,
so lost in horror are we.

I am not so stubborn that I argue
to oppose—that is not it at all.
Do not get in their mad truck
shuddering with flesh, screeching—
they will drive us to the abyss, I feel it coming—

Your cheeks are wet. I put my arms around you.
Mother! We share all suffering and all sorrow;
It is everywhere.
How many hours have disappeared
during this slow terror?

My stomach turns and growls,
my lips are cracked, my tongue is parched.
Ibrish's sister carried water in a pot
—from somewhere…

Oh, how difficult, difficult is breathing.
Dust! The air is choked with it
in this suffocating truck.

Chatip's grandfather lays unburied there.
Hatice weeps and tears her hair out.

Remember that day you spread butter on takos pite![2]
Butter floated on the bread like a ship until it melted!

Oh, mother, why do you wake me so early?
What will happen to our village,
our grapes and tobacco harvests (fruits of earth!),
how much I love the way leaves thicken the hills
after the snowmelt recedes.

Oh, why do you wake me so early?
Why don't you say anything to me now?
Why do you leave me and leave me?

You left me with this dead old man—
you left me in the terrible steppe,
I love you now and I will love you tomorrow
—but O my grief!

It is a cold inferno here, colder than when you woke me.
Why did you wake me up so early?
I loved you and I loved our land.
I longed for funeral prayers
but only one Elhamdü[3] and Amin were read.

Only the stars witnessed your burial.
Even the moon, so full of mourning, lost its orbit.
Soil groaned with your moon-blood and my tears.
Even the moon pitied the Crimean Tatar people
that night, and illuminated our ancient hills.
It made sun-prints in long exposures of the entire peninsula
and scripted on its surface the dictionary of our language.

Who says the moon and stars have no soul?
Stars scatter their photons carelessly—
We see everything in time.
The earth forgets everything in time.

But the person who issued the order
to break into our house and murder us—
What a creature! The kind of creature
who lives with such a thought
carries a withered, charred heart.

1   Qarakoz (Black-eyed)—a dog's nickname
2   Takos pite is a flat cake made without using butter in the dough
3   Elhamdü is a sura (chapter) from Fatıha, prayer

Aliye Kendzhe-Ali
Adapted by M.P. Carver

Cold Crimea

Cold Crimea—why do I love you?
Chill spring in your streets
and dying flowers on your trees—
like your enemy's bent thoughts
they hurt me, over and over...

Cold Crimea—my lot—Crimea,
you shake underneath my happiness.
My house is a prison without windows—
Even now, when you cannot breathe—
Why do I love you? Why love?

Homeland-lessness

Black clouds pour black snow,
Our elderly (No Homeland!) do not know happiness.
Our kids carry the wrong flag.
Our boys and girls—(No Homeland!) languageless.
Aging, windowless houses rot and stink.
Who have these walls seen and to whom have they been sold?
The arm and backs of our fathers (No Homeland!) were torn
Carrying stones, have not seen one bright day.
They light stoves, fiddle with ice water.
Youth and life are over, their faces wrinkled—
Our mothers, our mothers... (No Homeland!)—
A rusty nail driven into our living heart!

Crimea

Crimea is the stars in the sky,
I lie and watch.
"Qı–rım"[1] is written in the sky,
I read it there.
The weather is cool, tastes of fig,
smells of pear.
Crimea—we have one destiny,
Dzhankoy[2] and Uskut.[3]
Don't cry, Grandma,
the foreigners will leave soon.
Crimea is a gown made from stars
pulled on this week.
Our neighborhoods have calmed down,
our valley is narrow.
Crimea, one who truly loves you—
must be Crimean Tatar!

1 Qırım—Crimea
2 Dzhankoy—a city in Crimea
3 Uskut—a town in the Alushta region in Crimea

March 3, 2019

Today, inspiration won't come.
Today is like night for my people,
today my people fight
with a thousand-headed serpent,
that hides its face.
Today, my words don't hold up.
My Motherland is broken.
Everything has been overturned,
the houses left fatherless,
the kids left crying.
My poems will not be written.
My God, my people seek only
the mercy of your hands.
Save us from these fangs!
They tear my heart...

My Beloved

My beloved, my vast sea,
my unopened book,
my unwritten line.
My beloved, my bird flying far away,
my warm nest
on the cliff which cuts my hands.
My beloved, my world of one,
the sun for this one man, and
the struggle of that man...
My beloved, my day, my time, my each and every minute,
the destiny written on me,
my certain fire.

Seyare Kokche
Adapted by Lara Stecewycz

Scarlet Lands

Crimean land, how much you've undergone,
how many tears, troubles, and disasters you've seen,
how much blood has sunk into this land,
turned the black earth scarlet.

From scarlet rain, trees will grow,
the enemy who first stepped onto the scarlet earth will regret it—
whoever takes the land away will not live to see the morning.
The trace of the Crimean Tatars will not disappear.

Oh, my homeland, the person asking the question doesn't want the answer.
If everything repeats again and again, life will not change—
words on paper will not be wiped off for centuries,
time will not wait for those who fell behind.

The future is bright—there is no doubt. Winter doesn't last forever,
the man considering himself the owner wouldn't change his road,
spring will come, stranger's flags will stand proudly in the earth,
and in the blue sky, the yellow tamga[1] will be shining brightly.

1 Tamga—a national and cultural symbol, representing the Crimean Tatars'
   historical statehood, identity, and resistance to oppression

Didn't Conquer

Dedicated to Reshat Ametov and
other sheit ketken[2] compatriots

Interrogated, interrogated,
as if all the air
was sucked out of my lungs—
interrogated, tormented,
threatened with removal from Crimea,
with the removal of my blood,
leaking drop by drop—
tortured, murdered,
told to reject my homeland,
then buried beneath the scarlet earth—
murdered, murdered,
but you couldn't conquer. Didn't conquer!

2   *Sheit* or *shiit ketken* is a religious term referring to a person who died for a
good cause

I'll Never Understand

*Dedicated to Reshat Ametov and
other sheit ketken compatriots*

Those sharp words are as bitter as wind that freezes from the cold—
I cry from the cold.
It passes through your body, makes you shiver, throws you into zindan[3]
My heart shivers from the cold, aches from it, moans from it,
the cold has turned my veins to icicles
that gnaw at and torture my soul.
I run away
from the words, black thoughts
of killing humankind, torturing us—the other—
of terrible wishes, awful experiences…

How could you see these horrible things
and agree, my Allah? I don't understand.

3   Zindan—a prison built deep in the ground

Dialogue with the Sea

You come to me rarely
but I've been waiting for so long.
Strangers fill my shores, but not you...
Why? Did you forget me?
    I didn't forget my Sea, my Dear.
    If not to you, then to whom will I come?
    I see you in my dream
    I embrace your waves, and cry—
Who are these faceless people?
I'd been waiting for you—but they came instead!
    Oh, they are foreigners, strangers, enemies,
    those who are trying to make you their own.
No, it won't be like this any longer,
said the Sea, and turned black,
raising his waves to heaven, with all his might, then threw them ashore.
He destroyed other people's traces, licked off the land,
then quietly settled in my palm, silently dozed off.

My Heart Beats Like a Seagull

My heart beats
like a seagull
crying, tormented on the waves.
Drop by drop, salty drops of water
are dripping onto my torn heart
instead of medicine.
Drop by drop, salt water
touches me, running.

Wings are not saved from bitter winds,
the body of my Homeland
cries from suffering.
Black clouds shroud Crimea
as the invisible war continues

As if centuries are not enough,
our return does not end,
my people moan,
amazing green island
sinks into misery.
Be patient, my people,
the dawn will rise.

How many years, centuries—enough already!
spring will come to us too,
and freedom,
old people will see peace,
generations will flourish,
nights will become bright.
Just don't disappear, my people, the enemy will laugh!

My heart beats
like a seagull
crying, tormented on the waves.
Drop by drop, salty drops of water
are dripping onto my torn heart,
instead of medicine,
drop by drop, salt water
touches me, running.

My Crimea

Nataliya Shpylova-Saeed

"I did not forget my sea," writes Crimean Tatar poet Seyare Kokche. To which I would add: and neither have I. I visited Crimea for the last time a few years before Russia occupied the peninsula in 2014. By the time the Russians invaded, I had already settled in the U.S. As I followed the events rapidly unfolding in Ukraine, my memory kept turning to my childhood, so deeply intertwined with Crimea. While the international news focused on Russia's presence, little attention was paid to the region's indigenous population. Crimean Tatar voices were rarely featured on newscasts or even in the press. At the same time, Ukraine was often presented as a country that received Crimea as "a gift" from Khrushchev, which wasn't exactly the case. Most of the time, Crimea's many voices, diverse cultures, and entangled histories were dismissed.

I don't recall my first visit to Crimea—I was too young. My parents began taking my brothers and myself there for several weeks every summer soon after I was born. Traveling from my native city of Cherkasy in Central Ukraine to the Black Sea coast in the south of the country, we'd start out early, around 4 a.m. It's a little under five hundred miles from Cherkasy to Yalta, a resort city known for its hotels, restaurants, bars, and, of course, its luscious seafront. By early afternoon the same day, the Ayu-Dag Mountain, resembling a bear stretched out with its head touching the sea, would greet us.

This was in the pre-Google Maps era: my father relied on printed maps or his memory to get us to the destination. We explored many routes in hopes of finding better roads. But each time, no matter what route we chose, we enjoyed observing the changes in Ukraine's landscape: from forests to steppes, from flatlands to mountains, from rivers to the Black Sea. Trees offered a reliable roadmap, too. The assortment of apple and pear trees was gradually diversified by Ukraine's other treasures: sweet cherries, Kherson's watermelons, and then Crimea's peaches and grapes. The roads were lined with almond trees, vineyards, and fig trees. To a child used to sheltering apple trees and mystic mulberries, Crimea's palms and azaleas were out of a fairy tale. The architectural changes were nearly as dramatic. In the 1990s, more houses appeared built from blocks that looked like sun-dried clay-colored bricks—a signal of the return of Crimean Tatars. Their homecoming after more than half a century of exile to Central Asia was not easy, and the Ukrainian government could have done more for the people returning to their native land.

Once, arriving in Yalta, we couldn't find our hotel. My father stopped the car to ask locals for directions. A minute later, I heard him laughing and speaking with a stranger as if they were old friends. They hugged each other as they said goodbye. I wondered whom he had met. My father said the man had approached him: he noticed our car's license plate indicating Cherkasy Oblast. He was also originally from Cherkasy and was happy to run into visitors from the place of his birth.

In my mind, Yalta and Cherkasy remain part of one undivided nation, of my native land, of my childhood, and central to my identity. Today, the encounter that took place almost forty years ago symbolizes bonds by which many places in Ukraine—diverse and the same all at once—are interconnected.

In Crimea, we visited places charged with significant history, ancient and modern. The Livadia Palace, the site of the Yalta Conference in 1945, in which the fate of the post-war world was decided, has always been one of the regular destinations for travelers interested in history. We couldn't resist stopping by a place many locals criticized as touristy, and not at all representative of the essence of Crimea—the Swallow's Nest. But even the most critical visitors recognize the beauty—albeit turned into a commodity—of the white castle perched on a cliff overlooking the Black Sea. Looking down from the palace's observation deck is dizzying and breathtaking.

Crimea, with its layers of history, seduces. Built in the sixteenth century, the Bakhchysarai Palace, a residence of the Crimean Khans, combines Ottoman, Persian, and Crimean Tatar styles. I remember being drawn to the Fountain of Tears, but not because it was featured in the poem, which I was required to memorize in school. What captured my imagination was the past that the place contained. Crimea shelters a number of landmarks commemorating seminal moments in Ukrainian history. Prince Volodymyr the Great was baptized in Chersonesos, an ancient city in the southwestern part of the Crimean Peninsula, initiating the Christianization of Kyivan Rus'. The past is still visible, palpable. Here memory lives.

I made a promise to my husband: once Crimea is liberated, I will take him to the place that remains so dear and special to me, to that one place where the horizon is somewhat blocked by the trees but the glittering of the tantalizing coastline already promises the marvelous marine-scapes of the Black Sea. I remember my walks along the shore early in the morning and late at night. Every time, the sea is different: it soothes and it agitates, rather like history itself. It can lull you to sleep at night and hammer you awake in the morning. What never changes is a fragrance—salty, seaweedy, metallic, sandy—that cannot be found anywhere except Crimea.

We hope our collection of Crimean Tatar poetry and fiction helps readers—who may one day be free to travel to Crimea—to appreciate both its natural landscape, cultural entanglements, and the layers of history. Through their stories, our contributors share their hope that Crimea, one day, will be known to the world not because of Russia but for itself, for all that it has been: a home and a shelter to many cultures and multiple voices. For more than ten yeaers, Ukraine has been fighting Russia's incursion. The war is ongoing, and so is the struggle of the Crimean Tatars, who continue to defend their right to be at home in their own land.

Writers

Mustafa Amet was born in 1981 in Tashkent, Uzbekistan. In 1988, he and his family returned to Crimea. He graduated from the Department of Journalism at Marmara University (Istanbul, Turkey), and worked as a correspondent, editor, and presenter on the radio Meydan and the TV channel ATR in Crimea. He was the winner of the first Crimean Fig contest in the "Prose in the Crimean Tatar language" category. He is the head of the NGO, Institute for the Development of the Crimean Tatar Language.

Elmira Bekirova (Zekiye Ismailova, Tildzhan Sakla) was born in 1961 in the village of Koytash (Uzbekistan). From 1969, she lived in Tashkent, the capital of the Uzbek SSR, where she studied the Crimean Tatar language and literature at the Tashkent Pedagogical Institute and worked at the editorial office of the Crimean Tatar newspaper *Lenin bayrağı* (*Lenin Flag*). In 1990, she returned to Crimea and worked at the *Dostluq* (*Friendship*) newspaper. Now, she works at the editorial office of the *Qırım* (*Crimea*) newspaper. She is a winner of the "Crimean Fig" contest in the "Prose in the Crimean Tatar language" category.

Zera Bekirova was born in 1959 in the village of Kurgantepa, Uzbekistan. She graduated from the philology department at the Osh State Institute (Kyrgyzstan). She worked at the editorial office of the Crimean Tatar language newspaper *Yañı Dünya* (*New World*). During 2012-2018, she was the editor-in-chief of this newspaper. Since 2011, she has been the editor-in-chief of the women's magazine *Nenkecan*. She is the author of ten books, the main topic of which is the national movement of the Crimean Tatars, the deportation of 1944, and the folklore of the Crimean Tatar diaspora. Since 2011, she has been a member of the Union of Writers of Ukraine. She is a member of the Union of Eurasian Writers as well. She was the winner of the second "Crimean Fig" contest in the category "Prose in the Crimean Tatar language."

Aliye Kendzhe-Ali (Aliye Kendzhaliyeva) was born in 1986 in Uzbekistan. Two years later, her family moved to the homeland of their ancestors, Crimea. She started writing poems as a teenager. By education, she is a philologist and a pedagogue. Her prose and poetic works in Russian and Crimean Tatar languages were published in the *Qırım* (*Crimea*) and *Avdet* (*Comeback*) newspapers. She is also the author of the poetry collection *Feza* (*Cosmos*). She participated in the "Crimean Fig" contest and became one of the finalists.

Seyare Kokche (Seyare Useinova) was born in 1971 in Novorossiysk, Krasnodar Krai, Russia. At the age of 3, she returned to Crimea with her family. She is a philologist and choirmaster by education. She has academic publications on Crimean Tatar punctuation. She is an author of poetry and prose works, as well as a translator. Her poems and prose have been published in Crimean Tatar, Ukrainian, and Hong Kong newspapers and magazines including *Avdet* (*Comeback*), *Ukrainian Literary Gazeta*, *Yıldız* (*Star*), *Nenkecan*, *Fleurs des lettres* (*Flowers of the Letters*), and *Dzvin* (*Bell*). She is the winner of the 2018 "Crimean Fig" literary contest in the category "Translation from Ukrainian to Crimean Tatar," and a finalist in the category "Poetry in the Crimean Tatar Language."

Maye Safet (Maye Abdulganieva) was born in 1972 in Crimea (in the village of Rozdolne). She is the author of the collection *Yeşil kâinat* (*Green Universe*); and works as a translator and a literary editor. She has published her works in Crimean Tatar and Ukrainian magazines. She is the winner of the first "Crimean Fig" contest in the "Poetry in the Crimean Tatar language" category. Between 2020 and 2022, she was a member of the jury of the "Crimean Fig" contest and the editor of the Crimean Tatar part of the anthologies *Crimean Fig. Demirci* and *Crimean Fig. Çayır.*

Zulbiye Sattarova: At the request of the author, no biographical note is included.

Author of the Introduction

Alim Aliev is a journalist, human rights defender, curator of cultural and educational projects, essayist. He is also a member of Pen Ukraine. In 2018, he founded the Ukrainian-Crimean Tatar literary project "Crimean Fig" (Qırım İnciri), dedicated to the promotion of Crimean Tatar literature and culture in Ukraine and beyond. Alim Aliev serves as Ukrainian Deputy Director General of the Ukrainian Institute (affiliated with the Ministry of Foreign Affairs) and co-founder of CrimeaSOS. The books he authored include *Mustafa Dzhemilev: The Unbreakable* about the life of the Crimean Tatar leader. Alim Aliev serves as a participant and speaker of Crimean advocacy missions in the Council of Europe, European Parliament, OSCE, UN Security Council, and other political institutions.

Editors

Anastasia Levkova is a writer, journalist, and cultural manager. From September 2016 to April 2017, she presented a literary program on Crimean-Tatar Hayat radio titled "Radio Bookstore with Anastasia Levkova." She devised the principles for "Crimean Fig," the contest of writers and translators founded in 2018, for which she is a co-founder, coordinator, and a jury member. She is the author of four books, including *There is a Land Beyond Perekop: A Crimean Novel* (Laboratory, 2023).

Askold Melnyczuk has published four novels and a book of stories, *The Man Who Would Not Bow*. *The Venus of Odesa*, his selected poems, appears from Mad Hat in 2025. A volume of selected non-fiction, *With Madonna in Kyiv: Why Literature Still Matters (More than Ever)*, will be published by the Harvard Ukrainian Research Institute in 2026. He has edited a book of essays on the St. Lucian Nobel-prize-winning poet Derek Walcott and is also co-editor of *From Three Worlds*, an anthology of Ukrainian writers from the 1980s generation. Founding editor of Agni and Arrowsmith Press, he has taught at Boston University, Harvard, Bennington College and currently teaches at the University of Massachusetts Boston.

Nataliya Shpylova-Saeed is a memory studies scholar and literary critic. She teaches Ukrainian at Harvard University in the Department of Slavic Languages and Literatures. Her primary research interest is cultural memory, with a focus on Ukraine and Russia. She is the author of *Russia's Denial of Ukraine: Letters and Contested Memory* (Lexington Books Press, 2024).

Translators

M.P. Carver is a poet and visual artist from Salem, MA. She is Director of the Massachusetts Poetry Festival, and miCrO-Founder of *Molecule: a tiny lit mag*. Her work has appeared in *Rattle, Mantis*, and *Jubilat*, among others. Her second chapbook, *Hard Up*, is forthcoming from Lily Poetry in 2025.

David Earl is a writer and is currently enrolled in the Master of Fine Arts program for creative writing at UMass Boston, where he also works as a teaching fellow. In his spare time, he enjoys practicing calligraphy.

John Fulton is the author of four books of fiction, most recently *The Flounder and Other Stories* (Blackwater Press, 2023). His work has been awarded a 2024 NEA Fellowship in fiction and a Pushcart Prize, among other honors, and has appeared in *Ploughshares, The Missouri Review, The Sun, The Southern Review*, and *Zoetrope* among other venues. He is a professor at the University of Massachusetts Boston, where he currently directs the MFA program in creative writing.

Ha Jin is a poet and novelist. He mainly writes in English and has published poetry and fiction. Ha Jin has numerous awards, including Pen/Faulkner Award for Fiction, Pen/Hemingway Award for Debut Novel, and Flannery O'Connor Award for Short Fiction. His novel *Waiting* won the National Book Award in 1999. Ha Jin teaches at Boston University.

Hanna Leliv is a Ukrainian translator currently based in the US. She translates fiction and creative non-fiction, working between Ukrainian and English. From 2023 to 2024, Hanna Leliv was a Translator-in-Residence, Princeton University; during 2017–2018, she joined the University of Iowa's Literary Translation Workshop as a Fulbright Fellow. Her translations of contemporary Ukrainian literature into English have appeared in *Asymptote, BOMB, Washington Square Review, Circumference*, and elsewhere. Her translation of Markiyan Kamysh's *Stalking the Atomic City: Life among the Decadent* *and the Depraved of Chornobyl* was published in 2022. In 2024, in collaboration with Yevheniia Dubrova, Hanna Leliv translated *The Factory* by Ihor Mysiak, a Ukrainian writer who was killed in combat during the Russo-Ukrainian War.

Civitella and Yaddo alum **Diane Mehta** is the author of *Happier Far: Essays* (2025) and two poetry books: *Tiny Extravaganzas* (2023) and Forest with *Castanets* (2019). Her writing is in *The New Yorker, Virginia Quarterly Review, Kenyon Review, Harvard Divinity Bulletin*, and *A Public Space*. She is poet in residence with the New Chamber Ballet in New York City.

William Pierce's fiction has appeared in *Granta, Ecotone, American Literary Review*, and elsewhere. Excerpts from his manuscript *Twenty Sixteen have* appeared in Harvard Review, *The Western Humanities Review*, and *Literary Hub.* He is coeditor of AGNI and the author of *Reality Hunger: On Karl Ove Knausgaard's* My Struggle (Arrowsmith Press, 2016), a monograph first serialized as a three-part essay in *The Los Angeles Review of Books.*

Shuchi Saraswat's essays have appeared or are forthcoming in *Ploughshares, Orion, Michigan Quarterly Review*, and elsewhere, and have received special mentions in *The Best American Essays* and *The Pushcart Prize: Best of the Small Presses.* The senior editor of *AGNI*, she lives and works in Boston.

Leyla Seytkhalilova was born in Uzbekistan, where she pursued her studies at the Department of Foreign Languages at the State University. Later, she moved to Crimea, continuing her education in Crimean Tatar philology. Throughout her career, she taught at both the secondary and university levels and worked as a translator.

Lara Stecewycz is a Ukrainian-American poet from Massachusetts. She is a recent graduate of the Commonwealth Honors College at the University of Massachusetts Amherst and works as an Assistant Editor at Arrowsmith Press. She received the English Opportunity scholarship (2023), the Class of 1940 Prize in Poetry (2024), and a scholarship to attend the New York State Summer Writers Institute (2024). Her writing has been published in *The Massachusetts Review*, *Arrowsmith Journal*, and *Jabberwocky Journal*.

Shubha Sunder's debut novel, *Optional Practical Training*, will be released by Graywolf Press in March 2025. She is the author of *Boomtown Girl*, a story collection set in her hometown of Bangalore, India, that won the 2021 St. Lawrence Book Award and was a finalist for the Flannery O'Connor Prize for Short Fiction. Her writing has appeared in places like *Catapult*, *The Common*, and *Narrative Magazine*, and been shortlisted for *Best American Short Stories*. She lives in Boston with her family.

Acknowledgments

This collection would not have been possible without the generous and dedicated help of our colleagues and friends. We extend our deepest gratitude to everyone who reviewed the manuscript at various stages and collaborated with us in bringing this book to readers:

- **Translators' team:** M.P. Carver, David Earl, John Fulton, Ha Jin, Hanna Leliv, Diane Mehta, William Pierce, Shuchi Saraswat, Leyla Seytkhalilova, Lara Stecewycz, Shubha Sunder;

- **Arrowsmith team:** Nidia Hernandez, Julia Juster, Catherine Parnell, Gerard Robertson; and our appreciation to Ezra Fox, who was still part of Arrowsmith Press when we started our collection of contemporary Crimean Tatar literature;

- **Proofreaders:** Meia Geddes and Scott Aumont; and our special thanks to Lauren Thomas for reading the first versions of the translations;

- **Book cover artist:** Rustem Skybin

We extend our gratitude to Alim Aliev, Anastasia Levkova, and Leyla Seytkhalilova for their faith in this project and for entrusting us with the works of Crimean Tatar writers. We hope *Crimean Fig / Qırım İnciri* will make the world of Crimean Tatar culture and literature closer to Anglophone audiences.

Books by

ARROWSMITH
PRESS

Girls by Oksana Zabuzhko

Bula Matari/Smasher of Rocks by Tom Sleigh

This Carrying Life by Maureen McLane

Cries of Animals Dying by Lawrence Ferlinghetti

Animals in Wartime by Matiop Wal

Divided Mind by George Scialabba

The Jinn by Amira El-Zein

Bergstein
edited by Askold Melnyczuk

Arrow Breaking Apart by Jason Shinder

Beyond Alchemy by Daniel Berrigan

Conscience, Consequence: Reflections on Father Daniel Berrigan
edited by Askold Melnyczuk

Ric's Progress by Donald Hall

Return To The Sea by Etnairis Rivera

The Kingdom of His Will by Catherine Parnell

The Selected Poems of Oksana Zabuzhko
edited by Askold Melnyczuk

The Age of Waiting by Douglas J. Penick

Manimal Woe by Fanny Howe

Crank Shaped Notes by Thomas Sayers Ellis

The Land of Mild Light by Rafael Cadenas
edited by Nidia Hernández

The Silence of Your Name: The Afterlife of a Suicide by Alexandra Marshall

Flame in a Stable by Martin Edmunds

Mrs. Schmetterling by Robin Davidson

This Costly Season by John Okrent

Thorny by Judith Baumel

The Invisible Borders of Time: Five Female Latin American Poets
edited by Nidia Hernández

Some of You Will Know by David Rivard

The Forbidden Door: The Selected Poetry of Lasse Söderberg
tr. by Lars Gustaf Andersson & Carolyn Forché

Unrevolutionary Times by Houman Harouni

Between Fury & Peace: The Many Arts of Derek Walcott
edited by Askold Melnyczuk

The Burning World by Sherod Santos

Today is a Different War: Poetry of Lyudmyla Khersonska
tr. by Olga Livshin, Andrew Janco, Maya Chhabra, & Lev Fridman

Salvage by Richard Kearney

In the Hour of War: Poetry From Ukraine
edited by Carolyn Forché and Ilya Kaminsky

A Crash Course in Molotov Cocktails: Poetry of Halyna Kruk
tr. by Amelia Glaser and Yuliya Ilchuk

Don't Close Your Eyes by Hanna Melnyczuk

Tiny Extravaganzas by Diane Mehta

Departures from Rilke by Steven Cramer

On the Road to Lviv by Christopher Merrill
tr. into Ukrainian by Nina Murray

Nothing Bad Has Ever Happened
A Bouquet to Victoria Amelina

The Farewell Light by Nidia Hernández

Downfall of the Straight Line by Charles O. Hartman

The God of Freedom by Yulia Musakovska
tr. Olena Jennings and the author

Away Away by Mark Pawlak

The Miró Worm and the Mysteries of Writing by Sven Birkerts

St. Matthew Passion by Gjertrud Schnackenberg

New and Selected Poems by Glyn Maxwell

A Precise Chaos by Jo-Ann Mort

Where Do You Live? by Jennifer Jean

Coming Ashore by Thomas O'Grady

ARROWSMITH is named after the late William Arrowsmith, a renowned classics scholar, literary and film critic. General editor of thirty-three volumes of *The Greek Tragedy in New Translations*, he was also a brilliant translator of Eugenio Montale, Cesare Pavese, and others. Arrowsmith, who taught for years in Boston University's University Professors Program, championed not only the classics and the finest in contemporary literature, he was also passionate about the importance of recognizing the translator's role in bringing the original work to life in a new language.

Like the arrowsmith who turns his arrows straight and true,
a wise person makes his character straight and true.

—Buddha